GIRLS
CAN'T BE
KNIGHTS

Published by Myrddin Publishing
www.myrddinpublishing.com

First printing, June 2015

Girls Can't Be Knights is a work of fiction sited in a fictional version of the Pacific Northwest. People, places, and incidents are either products of the author's mind or used fictitiously. No endorsement of any kind should be inferred by existing locations or organizations used within it.

No horses, dogs, cats, crows, or bats were harmed in the making of this book.

ISBN: 978-1-68063-030-5

Cover copyright 2015 by Peter O'Connor

The Myrddin tree logo is a trademark of Myrddin Publishing and may not be reproduced without permission.

1/17

Amazon #15.

GIRLS
CAN'T BE
KNIGHTS

LEE FRENCH

unique electronic & print books

ACKNOWLEDGMENTS

I wish to thank the entirety of the Olympia Area Writer's Coop, all of whom have, in at least a small way, played a role in the production of this book. Special debts of gratitude belong to Connie, Irene, Shannon, Tricia, Tim, both Kaylas, and Melanie. In addition, I must thank Jo, Jeff, Matt, and Ruben for all being most excellent people.

Finally, Rachel and Yannick are both also fantastic people, and I wish you the best of luck on your respective journeys.

For Aiyre and Evan.

CHAPTER 1

CLAIRE

"No wonder nobody wants you."

The voice, belonging to a boy who barely knew her, made Claire freeze in the hallway. She had been content to walk away until then. Standing there, she heard the sniggers, snickers, and whispers that said they had an audience now. She clenched her hands into fists and she rounded on him. Storming back to him and his friends, she wanted to smack away that wide, smug grin plastered on his pretty face.

"Say that again," she dared him, her voice low and threatening.

"How cute." His grin changed to a sneer and his cool stare incensed her more. "Guys, look. This piece of ass—"

Her fist caught him under the chin, clacking his teeth together and jerking his head up. In rapid succession, she punched him in the kidneys and thrust her knee up between his legs. When he doubled over, she clasped her hands and drove her elbows down on his back. He curled up on the ground in front of her. With the crowd and his friends stunned into silence, she glared all around.

"Anybody else want a 'piece' of this?"

"What's going on here?" The teacher's voice broke the spell over the teenagers. Everyone suddenly had someplace else to be—except the boy's allies.

"This girl just snuck up on Brian and beat the crap out of him!" As Brian's buddy spoke, Claire noticed him tucking his cellphone out of sight. He'd probably filmed the whole thing. Later, if she looked, she'd undoubtedly find it online with the beginning edited off.

She didn't bother refuting him. No one would believe her. They never did. Instead, she shoved Brian with a foot and crossed her arms, glaring at the teacher and silently daring him to grab her arm or ear to drag her away.

The teacher obviously didn't recognize her, and she didn't know his name. "Boys, help Brian to the nurse's office. You can come with me to see the principal." He reached out for Claire, then thought better of it and pointed instead.

She marched to the front office with the teacher shadowing her every step. In a fit of petulance, she stopped at the door and refused to open it, but some other teacher foiled the gesture by exiting a second after she got there. Inside, the front office had a warm, homey feel. The decorations used the school colors of blue and silver, and included a cabinet with polished trophies from various events.

"Sit," the teacher snapped, pointing at a black plastic chair. He knocked on the door marked *Principal*. When he heard a voice tell him to come in, he left Claire under the watchful gaze of the secretary outside it. This thin, spindly woman had welcomed her five days ago with a warm, grandmotherly smile. Now, her stern frown made her think of a schoolmarm, the kind that would snap a ruler across your fingers if you dared whisper to your neighbor.

Claire dropped into the chair in a huff, crossed her arms, and refused to look at the secretary. Instead, she glared at the wall, picturing what would happen next and bracing for it. Getting thrown out of this school already would probably get her shoved into the alternative school, the one where all the troublemakers and pregnant girls go. That guy Brian shouldn't have said those things, though. He should've just kept his fat mouth shut.

The door opened and the principal followed the teacher out. Mr. Gary stopped in front of her. "Hello, Claire," he said in a Serious Principal Voice. "Come into my office, please."

Since he went to the trouble to say "please," she stood and did what he wanted, arms still crossed over her chest. Inside, she flumped down on one of his chairs and slid into a slouch.

Mr. Gary closed the door and sat in the black executive chair behind his large wood desk. He had a round, pleasant face with a prominent nose, and kind brown eyes. "Claire, I didn't think I'd been talking to you again so soon."

She grunted in acknowledgment because he left a pause that invited some kind of comment.

"I understand things are difficult for you." He clasped his hands on top of the desk, leaning toward her. "It's always hard to be the new kid transferring in during the middle of the school year. But Claire, fighting is never an appropriate response to anything."

She narrowed her eyes. "Am I just supposed to let people walk all over me?"

"No, of course not. But that doesn't make fighting acceptable."

"I thought this school had a 'zero tolerance' policy against bullying and harassment."

Mr. Gary took a deep breath and let it out slowly. "Claire, you've only been here for five days."

"Yeah, so I guess all that stuff Brian's been saying for three of them is nothing." She refused to meet his eyes.

"Claire, why did you throw the first punch?"

She rolled her eyes. These little chats always went exactly how she expected them to. "Whatever."

"I'm afraid I'm going to have to put a record of this incident in your file. In addition, you're going to write an apology to Brian."

That got her attention, and she stared at him, dumbfounded. "Excuse me?"

He set a blank piece of paper with the school's letterhead and a ball point pen on his desk, and pushed them toward her. "You're going to write an apology to Brian Avery, for hitting him without provocation."

"Without—" She jumped to her feet. "Do you have any idea what he's been saying to me? Of course not, because he always makes sure there are no teachers around. And his friends too!" She thumped his desk with both hands as she leaned forward. "Hey, Claire. Hey, look at me when I'm talking to you. Check out that nice piece of ass. I heard you'll spread those cheeks for anybody who asks. Hey, don't ignore me, bitch. No wonder nobody wants you." When she finished, her nostrils flared and she ground her teeth.

Mr. Gary frowned and his brow furrowed. "Did anyone else hear any of that?"

"Of course they did," Claire snarled. "Do you really think they're going to tell you about it, though? As if. Brian and his buddies are football jocks. They're popular and everybody likes them. Or pretends to."

He sighed and pushed the paper at her. "Claire, I'll check into your allegations personally, but it still doesn't excuse throwing the first punch. All you have to do is write out an apology for making the argument physical."

Outraged by the unfairness of this, and knowing exactly what Mr. Gary would discover when he "investigated," Claire snatched the paper and pen and stalked to the door. "Whatever," she growled.

"In addition," he said, his voice firm and hard, "you'll stay in the office for the remainder of the school day, and you're suspended for tomorrow. Come back on Friday."

"Just what I need," Claire snapped, "a day off to ponder my misdeeds." She stormed out, slamming the door behind her. Ignoring the secretary, she crumpled the paper into a wad and flung it and the pen away. Before anyone could stop her, she darted out the front door and ran. That jerk, blaming her for reacting to what Brian had said. That ass had gotten what he deserved. He would have to live with the knowledge that a girl beat him up, which suited her just fine.

The bell rang, signaling the end of lunch. Claire slipped through a break in the chain link fence separating the school from Grant Park. Someone startled her by hissing from behind a nearby tree. She spun and, when she saw who it was, put a hand to her chest to take a deep breath.

"Oh, it's you."

"Sorry, didn't mean to scare you." Drew yanked on the zipper of his backpack and shrugged it on. "Are you cutting class?" His shock of curly, red hair needed to be cut.

"Sort of. I just got suspended."

"Crap. What for? How long?" He pushed his glasses up his freckled nose and reached for her hand.

His honest concern cooled her anger, and she squeezed his hand. "Just tomorrow. For beating up that Brian guy on the football team."

"You should do what I do and steer clear of all of them." He squeezed her hand back and gave her a shy smile. "They don't matter. How long are either of us going to be at this school, anyway?"

"Yeah, I know. It's just not fair." How she would love to sit down and talk to Drew right now. For a wild moment, she met his gaze and had thoughts of dragging him along with her as she ran away. But he needed good grades as much as she did, and he had a better chance of getting them. "You should go. You're gonna be late for class."

"Oh, crap, yeah. Come back with me, Claire." He tugged on her hand, pulling her a step toward school.

With a shrug, she let go. "Nah. Bring my homework for me?"

"Yeah, sure." He stepped back to her and kissed her cheek.

She rubbed the spot, warmed and pleased, and watched him run off to class. When she switched homes, she usually had to meet all new kids. But once in a while, like this time, she wound up in the same place as someone she already knew. She and Drew had been in the same group home before. His presence gave her something to cling to, someone to trust and believe in. Besides, he was cute.

Hurrying through the park, she dodged around an adult she thought might be a gym teacher and jogged past the tennis courts. She slowed to a brisk walk once she left the grounds, aware that running stuck out like a red flag to cops watching for truants. Her favorite striped knee socks in red and black made her stand out enough already. Not knowing this part of the city well, she picked a direction and walked with her head up and a purposeful stride. The first rule of not getting caught: act like you belong and know what you're doing.

A dog barked at her as she strode down the street. It darted from its house until it reached the end of its chain. Churning up the grass on the edge of its front yard, it scrabbled to reach her and kept barking. She shied away from it and kept going. Three houses down, a cat on a low fence hissed at her and arched its back, scooting sideways with its tail up until it leaped at her. It scraped at her leg through her sock, making her squeal and stumble. She kicked to dislodge it and sprinted away. Another block down, a crow dived at her head, only missing because she happened to have paused to check her leg.

Either she'd accidentally walked through a spray of bacon perfume, or the entire world wanted to punish her by making all the local animals freak out. All she'd done was defend herself against a stupid bully. She knew how guys like Brian operated. He'd taunt her from a distance for a while, then after a few weeks, he'd find a way to get her alone. Every time she thought about that first time this kind of thing happened, she wished her father could still be around to glow with pride. He'd been the one who taught her how to throw a punch, after all.

Before he died. Before the fire. Before she'd lost everyone and everything that ever mattered. He'd promised to teach her how to swing the fake sword he used to act out battles with his friends. He'd promised to teach her to drive too, and lots of other things.

Crazed barking interrupted her thoughts and memories. This time, no chain stopped another lunatic animal. She stared in disbelief for a moment, then turned and ran for her life from this new demented dog. Dashing up the street with it chasing at her heels, she tripped over a curb and went sprawling, scraping her palms and knees. Ignoring the stinging, she scrambled to her feet and kept going.

Another cat darted out at her from nowhere, scraping through her sock with its claws, then hissing and falling back. She tripped again and staggered to collapse onto a park bench. Exhausted and confused, she curled up into a ball and gripped the locket under her shirt, hoping against hope that someone or something would make all this stop.

CHAPTER 2

JUSTIN

Tariel's silver hooves clopped along the city streets. On her back, Justin held a paper map, checking the street signs as he tried to follow their progress with his finger. "Unless we're really lost, it should be the next left."

"That's what you said at the last intersection." The horse's words sounded like a whinny to anyone else.

"I know, but this time I'm sure." He folded up the map and stowed it in the back pocket of his jeans. "One of these days, I'm going to get the hang of this job. And then I'll be *dangerous*."

"The world trembles in anticipation." The mare raised her head and pranced.

Justin noticed a cluster of people with cameras and cellphones pointed at him. Knowing he presented a perfect picture of a knight in shining armor, he waved with a jaunty smile. Tariel's power stirred up around him, fluttering his long, emerald-green cloak in a breeze and shining a ray of bright light on the pair of them. The effect gave his audience a flash of his green-tinted chainmail and pauldrons while downplaying his work boots and jeans.

"I see a sign for the place," Tariel said, "so we've mysteriously wound up where we meant to go. It's a miracle."

Under the scrutiny of onlookers, he refrained from thumping her between the ears for her cheek. "Where I come from, we call that sass, and I get plenty from my wife. You can stuff it."

"You married her, so I assumed you like it."

"*You* can be an ass if you want. I'll pass."

"Oh, your wit is rapier-sharp today."

"Funny." He pulled on the reins to get her to stop in front of the Oregon Historical Society. It sat on a one-way street, across from a strip of green space. Statues and park benches lined a concrete path between trees and strips of grass. "Wait here and don't cause any trouble."

"No, of course not. That's your thing."

Justin rolled his eyes and hopped down from the saddle. "There isn't one person in my life who respects me," he groused as he jogged across the street. "Not even one. Wife, two daughters, horse, boss, in-laws, every single one a smartass or a tyrant."

Three brickwork steps brought him up to the museum entrance, and he took a deep breath. The glass double doors opened into a wide atrium with regal blue carpet bordered by brick flooring. To the side, a tall, skinny man stood behind the lobby counter that held a cash register, pamphlets, and a poster Justin barely glanced at. He ignored the man and strode deeper into the museum, past a small shop with a wall of bookshelves and displays of knickknacks and jewelry.

"Excuse me," the man called after him, polite yet stern. "There's an admission charge for this museum."

Justin sighed and glanced over his shoulder. Thankfully, the guy hadn't emerged from his post to follow him. "I'll just be a minute. My wife thinks she dropped something upstairs." For good measure, he added a genial wave.

No alarms or sirens went off, and the cashier didn't chase after him. Justin hurried the rear of the building and noted another exit by the stairs. Kurt had asked him to find a specific hat on the second floor, which meant going up past memorabilia from the 1940s and 50s hanging on the walls. He reached the upper floor and plunged past a display about Native American influence on the Pacific Northwest. Next, he passed through the Lewis and Clark Expedition exhibit, some Roaring Twenties memorabilia, and a World War II section.

The exhibits had been arranged in a loop, putting him at the stairs again. Only then did he stumble across a glass display case of hats, gloves, shoes, purses, and scarves, all from the early half of the twentieth century. With more than two dozen hats to choose from, he frowned. At least the display helpfully included descriptions. Kurt had said it would be a "ladies' hat with the indelible stamp of post-war Portland." When pressed for more information, he'd shrugged and shooed Justin out to go get it done.

Movement in his peripheral vision made him turn to look. A mother with two young boys edged her sons around him without bothering to check the display. He got that reaction a lot. Some people wanted to touch his armor, some asked for his picture, and some treated him like a plague carrier. Ignoring them, he ran his gloved fingers over the board, reading the dates and descriptions.

Two hats fit his instructions—the rest claimed to be men's hats or from the 30s or earlier. He had to choose between a rounded white hat with a white silk scarf tied around it in a bow, and a pink, wide-brimmed floral hat. The white one had a heart design in the weave of the scarf, and a description of "woman's dinner hat." Cheerful silk roses and beads festooned the other hat, offering so much more flair than its description of "woman's picture hat" suggested.

Eyes flicking from one to the other, he shrugged. "Portland *is* the city of roses," he muttered. Having made a choice, he knocked a fist on the glass to test its strength. They'd chosen a sturdy, reliable pane, probably safety glass to avoid damaging the pieces within. He gripped the hilt of the sword hanging from his belt and scanned the entire case to pick the best place to cut it open.

In the upper corner of the side panel, he noticed a square black plastic piece and pushed on it. The magnet inside it released, letting him swing the panel open. He smiled, pleased he wouldn't have to destroy anything. With luck, no one would even realize he'd taken the hat before he returned it.

"Hey, what are you doing?" Justin had managed to get partway into the case and stretch his arm out to touch the hat before the voice interrupted him. It belonged to a gentleman in a suit with a patch identifying him as private security.

"Nothing." Justin snatched the hat and ducked away just in time to avoid the guard's attempt to grab him. As expected, when the guard snatched at his cloak, the man's fingers slid over it without finding any purchase. Running down the stairs, Justin heard the guard reporting a theft on his radio. Just what he needed.

Tucking the hat under his cloak, he hurried out the side door and sprinted through the plaza beside the building, then vaulted over the low iron fence separating it from the wheelchair ramp. He hoped it would take the cops at least a few minutes to respond to a report of a weirdo taking an antique hat.

CHAPTER 3

CLAIRE

A strange noise made Claire look up through tears she hadn't been able to prevent. She saw a white horse standing in the sunshine, light forming a halo around the mare and hooves glinting silver. The horse held a cat in its teeth and flung it away, then huffed and nodded her head at Claire, giving the bizarre impression she had done that to help. Swiping her arm across her eyes to dry them, Claire swore as she remembered she'd been wearing makeup. The long sleeve of her tie-dyed shirt, already streaked with blood from her scrapes, now had smears of black eyeliner and purple eye shadow across the white and blue pattern. Her face would be even worse.

The horse danced in place and whickered at her, then lifted a leg and struck a majestic pose, her blue eyes rolling upward and back down at her. Drawn by the movement, she noticed the statue on the block of stone the horse stood in front of. Some guy on a horse had been set up there, and this real horse had taken the exact pose of the statue. She stared in disbelief for a second, then had to laugh at the absurdity.

"Showboat," chided a male voice behind her. "Come on, let's go."

Claire turned to see the owner of the voice and had no idea what to make of him. The man, well built and muscular, jogged toward them in green-tinted chainmail with green steel pauldrons over jeans and work boots, an emerald-green cloak streaming out behind him, and a sword strapped to his waist. Her father had dressed like that sometimes—exactly like that. This guy might have known him, or might know his friends.

In direct contrast with his tall, dark, and handsome knightly figure, he carried a pink, old-fashioned ladies' hat with fake flowers and a wide brim. From the way he handled it, she guessed it must be important or expensive. Claire had no idea what to make of that, as the hat also didn't look new. When she glanced behind him, the sign for the building he'd just come from read *Oregon Historical Society.*

The man shook his head with a roll of his eyes for the horse, and beckoned the mare toward him. "Don't be a pain, we need to get out of here. They didn't exactly *want* me to have it."

Stamping a hoof, the horse snorted and nodded at Claire.

Turning, the man peered at her, making her blush. He gave the horse a sidelong glance, and the mare nodded again, as if to say she wouldn't cooperate unless he did something. With a shrug, the man smiled at Claire. "Hey. You look like you're having a rough day, and are probably tired. Can we give you a lift someplace?"

She opened her mouth to tell him to go away, but only managed to croak out an unintelligible noise. After coughing to clear her throat, she heard the wail of a police siren in the distance and gulped. "Um, sure."

He offered her a hand and pulled her to her feet. "I'm Justin."

"Claire."

"You ever ride a horse before, Claire?"

Her attention shifted to the magnificent beast as he patted the mare on the neck. She gulped again. "Yes, but it's been a while."

"I'll climb up first. You put your foot on mine, give me your hand, and jump up. I'll pull. You'll sit in front of me. Okay?" His voice came out gentle and pleasant, and she wondered if he had any idea how much she missed having someone, anyone, talk to her like that. Everyone else who was "nice" to her did it out of pity, but she could tell Justin's offer came from something else. Sympathy, maybe, or just a sense of decency. It made her eyes sting again.

Nodding, she wiped her face and followed his instructions. His strength proved more than enough to get her into the saddle in front of him. Sitting on this strange man's lap felt creepy, and even more so when he handed her the hat and put his arms around her to manage the horse's reins. Somehow, though, he gave her the same sense of security and warmth that her father always had.

"Hold onto her mane if you need to," his voice rumbled in her ear. He turned as the sirens screamed closer, muttered, "Crap," and snapped the reins.

She clutched the hat to her chest and grabbed a handful of white horse hair as the beast lunged into action. The mare's hooves clanged on the concrete and they dashed past a statue of Abraham Lincoln. Leaning back to look behind them earned her a nudge.

"Move with us, not against us," Justin warned, his mouth close to her ear. "Yes, there's cops chasing us. It's not a big deal."

Claire wanted to ask if he'd stolen the hat, but she already knew the answer. He seemed so nice, then he had to go and be a criminal. A thief and a truant rode a horse up Park Avenue—it sounded like the start to a bad joke. They turned and left the green strip behind, galloping up a city street. The horse dodged cars and pedestrians alike as it danced between asphalt and sidewalk. People stared and pointed. A few fumbled for their phones to take pictures or video.

Several blocks later, the sirens had faded into the distance, unable to follow them through traffic. "Where do you live?" His voice startled her after he'd been silent for so long, obviously concentrating on their escape.

"Oh, uh." If she told him, he'd deposit her there. The cops would come and pick her up. She'd get an earful from Brad, her social worker, and then he'd spend the rest of the evening trying to persuade the foster parents at her current group home to give her a second chance. Either she'd spend the night in a holding cell because they had nowhere else to put her, or she'd go back there. Both choices sucked. "Nowhere."

"Nowhere? Really?"

"Yeah. Really."

"Huh. Okay. Hm." He hauled on the reins to get the horse to turn down a pedestrian walkway and they sped up. "I don't believe in coincidences, so you can come home with me tonight."

She flushed, wondering if he'd tricked her with the fatherly demeanor. "Um, I...can't, uh, pay you or anything."

Justin chuckled. "Don't worry about it. If we ever let a lack of money stop us, we'd be dead already. Tariel, take us home."

The strange word confused her until she realized it must be the horse's name. Her father's horse had had a strange name too: Kupiri. This mare, though, looked nothing like his stallion. That huge brute had been chestnut-brown with shiny black hooves and eyes. Still, so many similarities made her ask, "Did you know Mark Terdan?"

The horse's ears flicked back.

"Name sounds familiar, sure."

He'd said he didn't believe in coincidences, and she had a feeling she shouldn't, either. At the moment when she'd needed someone to come and rescue her, a knight appeared and did it. If her father were alive, he would have done the same thing. In fact, she could picture him bringing a stray teenager home for dinner and offering her a place to sleep.

The horse taking a freeway on-ramp surprised her. They galloped up Interstate 205, staying in the breakdown lane on the right side. Tariel sped up enough that Claire screwed her eyes shut and cringed away from the wind. Justin curled an arm around her and held her close. Something cut the wind down, and she cracked an eye open to see he'd pulled his cloak around to cover her. It filled the small space with the scent of vanilla and something woody, like cedar. Looking down, she could see the road speed past, and she wondered how fast they were going. Justin hadn't ducked under the cloak with her, and she wondered how he managed to avoid getting bugs in his eyes and mouth.

The cloak flapped up, showing her they'd reached the I-205 bridge. Sunshine flashed on the water as they kept going. This ride felt ridiculous, magical, insane. Not two hours ago, she'd sat in the school cafeteria by herself, ignoring the stares from Brian, his buddies, and the pack of girls who fawned all over them. If they could see her now...they'd probably still find a way to be jerks.

At least she didn't have to go to school tomorrow. Maybe, if Justin and whoever he lived with were nice, she could talk them into letting her stay until Friday morning. A wild hope bloomed in her chest as she thought of being able to find a permanent home. No more group homes, no more three month stays with a couple or family who had no idea what to do with her, no more social workers. The shrink visits would probably continue, but they never bothered her much. Spending an hour talking and thinking about herself was fine.

She watched the water give way to land, then water again, then back to land. Tariel took them off the freeway three exits into Vancouver, Washington, and Justin pulled the cloak off Claire. The last time she'd been here, her father had to stop for gas on the way home from a family visit to Mount St. Helens. It looked about the same as Portland, as far as she could see. They trotted down city streets, heading east. The horse seemed to know where to go, and Justin didn't steer so much as hold on.

They kept going and going. The city thinned into suburbs, then they turned down a street and saw nothing but trees and shrubs. Tariel sped up again, turning down another street. From there, they took an unpaved road that led to a faded red house squatting among the trees with an ancient white truck parked in front of it. Well-tended gravel paths led deeper into the property. Scalloped white trim and a tidy flower and herb garden created the impression of a welcoming, friendly farmhouse.

When Tariel stopped next to the truck, Justin helped Claire climb off the horse, then hopped down beside her. "Welcome to the Brady Farm."

"It kinda reminds me of the place where I grew up," Claire said with a wistful sigh.

Justin smacked Tariel on the rump. "I'll be out later," he told the horse. Giving Claire a smile, he held out his hand. "Can I have the hat back?"

"Oh, yeah. Sorry." She shoved it at him, and he took it. "What do you farm here?"

"Me? Nothing." He beckoned for her to follow him down the path to the left. "The in-laws keep goats and pigs and chickens, and they grow vegetables. If you go a short way from the house, you'll run into an apple orchard, and there's a cranberry bog and a blueberry thicket." They passed through a clearing with an old, dead stump in the center and a lean-to against the wall of the farmhouse filled with neatly stacked firewood. An axe lay under it, and a few dozen logs still in need of splitting had been left in a pile.

Beyond the clearing was a smaller house, this one painted green with bright white trim. It had its own garden, with orange flowers around the edge and most of the plants cut back. Claire guessed they'd been vegetables until a recent harvest. Justin led her to the door and wiped his boots on the mat before walking in without knocking.

"Come on in," he said, holding the door for her. She entered a small mud room and slipped her cheap old sneakers off while Justin unlaced his boots and left them behind. He hung his cloak on one hook and his sword belt on the next. The hat went on the same hook as the cloak. He opened the inner door for her. "I'm home," he called through it. "I brought a guest."

They walked into a tiny kitchen made smaller by a round table with four chairs in the middle of it. Claire figured the scratched and dented white appliances must be older than her, and the decorating too. Peeling pale yellow wallpaper with a tiny, dingy white, heart pattern clashed with the brown and white linoleum and the white-speckled, golden-yellow countertop. When it had all been new, it had probably matched and created a pleasantly warm room.

No wall divided the kitchen from the family room. The linoleum stopped and beige carpet began, the wallpaper stopped and wood paneling began. A sagging brown couch sat opposite a boxy TV resting on stacked metal milk crates whose open sides served double duty as bookshelves. Fuzzy pink blankets lay everywhere, along with pink and lavender dolls and stuffed animals. Two young girls erupted from the explosion of girly toys, both in homemade, satiny princess dresses, and ran to Justin.

Claire noticed pictures on the walls of these two girls and of the beautiful woman who walked in through the door leading deeper into the house. The family portrait, with Justin sitting and holding his daughters close while his wife hugged his shoulders from behind, struck her heart. She remembered a similar picture on her family's wall, a photo she no longer had. The sight of it made her rub a thumb over her locket.

Justin picked up both girls, one in each arm. "This is Claire. Tariel found her, and she needs a place to stay tonight. Claire, this is Missy." He nodded to the toddler with white-blonde curly hair. "And Lisa." The older girl also had blonde hair, in waves instead of curls. "And this is Marie, my wife." Like Justin, Marie didn't seem old enough to have two kids, a house, and responsibilities. At most, Justin couldn't be older than twenty-five, and his wife had to be younger than that.

"Goodness." Her face drawn with concern, Marie went to Claire and put an arm around her shoulders. Wisps of platinum-blonde hair that had escaped from her ponytail brushed against Claire's cheek. "Had a rough day, it looks like. Let's get you cleaned up."

Marie's concern made everything hurt again. Claire's leg throbbed, her hands stung, and her eyes ached. She nodded and let Marie escort her to a bathroom in the back. After pulling out some towels, bandages, and ointment, Marie left her alone in the tiny room. She shut the door, leaving Claire staring at herself in the mirror. The smeared makeup and blood made her look like a strung-out tramp. Panic warred with hope in her mind and both tangled with confusion. How did today turn into this? What would tomorrow be like? She had no idea.

It would take an awful lot of soap to wash all this away.

CHAPTER 4

JUSTIN

"Daddy, will you play?" Missy leaned against his shoulder.

Lisa wriggled to get down. "We're having a tea party."

Justin crouched and set Lisa's feet on the floor. Two years ago, when Lisa turned three and Missy joined the family, he resigned himself to tea parties, unicorns, princesses, and pink. Any other day, he'd accept the invitation and enjoy the time with his daughters. "Sorry, I can't right now." Pulling Missy away from him required firm conviction and not looking at her big eyes and skilled pout. "I have to go see Kurt, and then I have to change out of my armor."

Missy sniffled, signaling the start of a bout of fake crying that he didn't have time to deal with right now. "Daddy, play," she whined.

Fixing his attention on Lisa as he pried the toddler from his side, he sighed. "Can I count on you both to help me out with something important?"

Missy stopped pouting and set her feet on the floor, gazing at him with interest and adoration. Lisa perked up and gave him her attention too.

He smiled at them both. "Claire is sad right now because some bad things happened to her this morning. If she comes out before I'm back, can you see what you can do to cheer her up a little?"

"Yes, Daddy." Both girls gave him solemn nods.

"I knew I could count on you." He pulled a glove off and tousled Missy's hair. Marie had returned to working on dinner and he went to her side. Leaning in to kiss her cheek, he told her, "I'll be back in a few minutes."

Marie nodded. "Who is she?"

"A kid I found in Portland who needed help. She can sleep on the couch tonight."

"Jay," Marie said with a frown in her voice, "you can't just pick up stray teenagers and bring them home. She's not a puppy."

"Tariel found her. I can't explain why, but I feel like I have a connection to her somehow."

She took her attention away from the bowl she'd been whisking and gave him a mild look of concern and suspicion. "Oh. Really."

He snorted, then kissed her ear and brushed it with his nose. "Not like that. More like kinship: a sister or a daughter. Besides, she's maybe fifteen, and I've already got plenty of woman right here." He rubbed her butt and brushed his thigh against hers.

"Mmhmm." She turned and kissed his nose. "Make sure you remember that, Sir Knight."

"Yes, My Lady."

She nudged him away with her hip. "Go on, Kurt is waiting."

He pushed his leg against her, unwilling to leave yet. Holding her cheek, he kissed her. She deserved to be kissed, often and with interest. He offered it as a small token of his appreciation whenever he could. Besides, Kurt *could* wait and so could the rest of the world.

Marie broke it off before he wanted her to and smiled at him. "You're forgiven. Get moving. Dinner will be ready in half an hour."

He brushed his thumb down her cheek and grinned, pleased to have put that sparkle in her eyes. After slipping on rubber boots in the mud room, he grabbed the hat and jogged up the gravel path, then through the wood-chopping clearing. Instead of heading to the farmhouse, he plunged into the trees. Stupid bad luck made him need a quiet, forested spot to go see Kurt. He hopped over bulging roots and skirted shallow mud pits with practiced ease.

Five minutes of jogging later, he stopped beside an old sycamore with a tattered yellow ribbon hanging from the lowest branch. The place had proven perfect every time, and he'd tied that ribbon five years ago himself. Back then, he'd wandered for hours to reach a spot that worked for him. Now, he'd been here so many times he could find it blindfolded.

Holding his hand out, he took a deep breath and let the rich, earthy scent of the dirt, moss, and trees wash over him. With a tiny effort of will, he flexed his fingers open in a sharp movement and watched as the expected small white spark flared into existence two feet in front of him. It grew until it filled his vision, then he stepped forward.

His rubber boot hit stone and his vision cleared to show him the Palace. This room, with a battered old armchair and thick mattress on a cot, belonged to him. No one else could ever enter it unless he allowed them to. So he'd been told, anyway, and nothing had ever proved that wrong. He checked the shelves lining the wall and found everything in order. To be on the safe side, he always kept a change of clothes, a spare pair of boots, and a stack of books here.

Not caring about leaving muddy tracks on the woven rug and stone floor, he crossed the room to the main door and strode out into the hallway. Doors lined the stone corridor, each made of something different. His happened to be sycamore wood, with the number 557 burned into it and painted with silver. The door opposite had been assembled from old car parts; Mr. 556 had found his doorway in a junkyard.

In something of a hurry, Justin jogged up the hall to the central hub of the dormitory wing and hopped down the stairs to the fourth floor. Kurt lived in number 462, behind yellow aluminum siding with cedar shingles. The lucky bastard had found his doorway for the first time inside his own house.

Justin rapped on the door and tossed it open. "I got the hat."

"Come in, come in," Kurt wheezed from around the corner.

All the rooms in the dormitory had the same flag shape and size, and the same stone floors and walls. The old man sat in his wide, reclining chair, covered by a blanket. When Justin, then a fresh-faced, eighteen-year-old idiot, had first met Kurt, the older man had already slowed down and couldn't do the job anymore. Over the years, he'd shriveled and lost mobility. He lived here permanently now. His children and grandchildren could have taken him in, but he preferred not to be a burden on them while he waited to die.

Justin brought the hat to the frail old man's side and set it on his hand. "I think they want it back."

"They can have it when I'm gone," Kurt sneered. He clasped the brim with gnarled fingers and closed his eyes with a sigh. "My poor Emmy." His shaking arm lifted the hat to his nose and he inhaled deeply. "It still smells like her. She used lavender soap on her hair. Anna went and gave it away without even asking me."

Justin crouched at Kurt's side and patted his knee. "I'm sure she thought she was doing the right thing. Why'd you want it now, though? It's been there for a while."

Kurt sighed and sniffed the hat again. "I want to make an illusion of her before I go, of how she looked when I first met her. All I can remember of her is a saggy old broad that smelled like cookies. But what a gorgeous dame she was back then. That Liz Taylor tramp couldn't even come close to my Emmy. None of those movie star hussies could."

"She sounds like a knockout."

"Damned straight, she'd knock you out. Leave you lying on your rump for a day with how stunning she was."

Chuckling, Justin stood up. "I've got to get back. We've got company tonight. Keep the hat as long as you like."

"Not as if you could take it from me, you hulking brute."

"Nope, I sure couldn't. You'd throw me over your knee and give me a spanking for even trying."

"You know it, boy, and don't you forget it."

CHAPTER 5

CLAIRE

If she stopped to think, Claire might wind up crying in the bathtub. She tossed her shirt at the door and washed her face and all the scratches and scrapes. When she checked herself in the mirror again, after using soap and hot water, her face seemed plain and ordinary. This was the Claire who woke up every morning and sat down and tried to change herself with makeup. Why did she do that? Her shrink might say she didn't like Ordinary Claire for some reason. Exotic Claire was more interesting, more mysterious, more capable of punching stupid boys in the face for being jerks.

Someone knocked on the door. "Are you okay in there?" Marie's muffled voice held genuine concern.

"I dunno." The words slipped out of her mouth. She wanted to take them back. "I mean, yeah."

After a long pause, Marie said, "I can wash the blood out of everything. Just bring it to the kitchen. I'm leaving a spare shirt hanging on the doorknob."

"Okay, thanks. I'll be out in a minute." She realized that a small place like this probably only had the one cramped bathroom, and she'd been tying it up for the past ten or fifteen minutes. They had a training potty in here with the toilet, and a toddler out there who might need to use it at any moment. She rubbed her face with the towel and opened the door a crack to grab the fresh shirt to throw it on. Unwilling to leave a mess, she picked up after herself, carrying the dirty shirt and towel out.

Back in the family room, she found Justin sitting on the couch with his daughters on his lap, wearing a faded green T-shirt instead of his armor. Lisa held a pink book with sparkly blue lettering up for him, and he read it to them in an animated voice, telling them about a kitten's misadventure with a ball of yarn. Bespelled by the sight, she stopped and leaned against the wall, listening to his baritone voice rumble the words of a story he couldn't possibly be interested in. Like her father had done for her and her little brother.

Marie took the towel and shirt, breaking the spell and causing Claire to follow the older woman into the kitchen. Marie tucked the bundle in a corner and pulled a pot out of a cabinet. "Are you allergic to any foods?" She set the pot in the sink and turned the water on to fill it.

"What? Oh. No. I can eat whatever." Claire stood there, watching her fetch squash and broccoli and an onion. These people had taken her in, no questions asked, and now intended to feed her and give her a place to sleep. They did this without the state assigning her, without anyone paying them to, without knowing anything about her except that she needed help, without demanding—or even just asking for—anything in return. Her eyes stung again.

That first foster home had been like this. Except then, she'd been too wrapped up in grief for them to handle. Claire took a step forward. "Um, can I help or anything?"

Marie gave her a dazzling smile. "Sure. Here." She offered Claire the cutting board and knife, asking without words for her to take over chopping vegetables. "I'm just going to make a quick stir-fry. Do you like noodles or rice better?"

"Rice, I guess." She picked up the knife and attacked the onion.

"Justin said you're from Portland?" As Claire cut things, Marie took them away and added more.

"Outside it, actually. Originally. I live in Portland now, though."

"Just you? Not your family?"

"Yeah. Just me." Claire's eyes teared up, and she decided to blame the onion. "My parents, um, they died. A while ago."

"Oh, I'm sorry. You must be in the system, then." Like Justin, she managed to sound sympathetic instead of pitying. It struck her as so odd and comforting, she couldn't help but like Marie.

"Yeah. About six years." Wiping her eyes on the back of her hand, she sniffled. "Were you in it?"

"No, not me." She pointed over her shoulder. "Justin. When he fell for me, my parents took him in here. This is their farm. He was removed from his home, though. His dad is still alive."

"Oh." Claire had no idea which was worse and didn't really want to know the details. "He seems like a really great dad."

"Yes." Marie smiled warmly. "He made an effort to learn how to be one. My dad is a pretty good role model on that front."

Claire looked over at Justin and his two girls. He'd finished the book and now fell to tickling them both until they shrieked. He then picked Missy up, threw her over his shoulder, and carried her into the kitchen. Peering into the pot, he grinned. "This looks kinda like it needs some meat."

Missy giggled and kicked her bare feet. "I'm a moo!"

"I don't know," Marie said with a wink for Claire. "That one's kind of small. Maybe we should fatten her up a bit more first."

"You sure? I bet she's delicious."

"Moo! Moo!"

Claire struggled to figure out if this bothered her or inspired her, and settled on giving them all a weak grin as the antics played out. She turned away from them and focused on the vegetables. Zucchini didn't remind her of anything in particular. Her mother had never asked her to help in the kitchen. Everything she knew about cooking came from learning to fend for herself. To her relief, the game ended before she finished chopping things. Justin kissed Marie on the cheek and said he'd be back in a few minutes, then left the house.

Marie put a hand on Claire's arm. "Would you mind sitting with the girls while he's out?"

"Oh. Uh." The request caught her off guard. "Aren't you worried I'm... I dunno, mean? Or an idiot. Crazy. An axe murderer or something."

"I trust Justin's judgment." Her mouth fell into a lop-sided grin as Claire lifted an eyebrow. "Most of the time."

"Uh-huh. This is the same guy who rides a horse on the freeway."

Marie laughed. "Yes, well. He's got a good heart. You don't have to really do anything, just keep them over there with their toys."

"I guess. I'll give it a shot." She surrendered the knife and took a deep breath. Facing two little girls obsessed with pink and princesses seemed scary for some reason. Maybe it was only because she hadn't been that girl for a long time. "Hi," she said as she picked her way to the couch, taking care to avoid stepping on any of their things.

Both girls gave her wary smiles as she sat down. After a few moments of awkward silence, Lisa leaned over and touched a red stripe with one small fingertip. "Where did you get these socks?"

The simple question surprised her. In Lisa's place, Claire thought she'd ask prying questions to figure out why her dad brought a stranger home. "There's this store in Portland that only sells socks. They have all kinds of colors and patterns. You can even get two socks that don't match as a pair."

Lisa's big blue eyes went wide. "Why would you do that?"

Claire shrugged, not sure about the answer. "To be weird, I guess. Different. Fitting in is great and all, but you gotta be yourself."

Nodding with utter solemnity, Lisa withdrew her finger and offered Claire a plush doll made from scraps of cloth sewn together and stuffed, with an equally patchy dress. "You don't have a doll, so you can have this one."

Surprised by the gesture, Claire took it and remembered a doll she'd had at Lisa's age. Her mother had gotten it for her from a catalog, with brown eyes and silky black hair like her own. For whatever reason, they couldn't get the tanned skin tone right. She'd set it on a shelf and not played with it much.

"This is a really cool doll. Does she have a name?"

"Yes, but she's yours now, so you can name her whatever you want."

A lump formed in Claire's throat. She didn't deserve a gift, especially not one made by hand for someone else. "No, that's not how stuff works. Everybody keeps their first name even though they might get a new mom. And really, I'm just borrowing her anyway, since...I guess I need one while I'm here?"

"Do you have a doll at your house?"

"Um, no."

"Then you can keep her and take her home so you have one all the time."

Claire stared at the girl, uncomprehending. "Wait. You're giving me your doll? For real? Why?"

Missy grabbed her skirt and used it to climb onto the couch and sit beside her. "Claire sad."

Lisa shrugged and picked up a stuffed white horse with patchy, worn fur. She clicked her tongue for clopping noises as she bounced it along the edge of the couch.

"I'm not sad. I mean, not really. I just—g" She frowned at the doll. "Your dad is pretty awesome and he makes me miss mine."

"Where's your daddy?"

Claire sighed and sat back on the couch, choosing not to push the memory away. "Once upon a time, there was a princess." English was her worst subject, so she had no idea how to carry this story along in a way they wouldn't find disturbing. The girls, though, gave her their rapt attention, so she felt compelled to try. "She lived in a house kind of like this one. It was bigger, though, with a second floor above. She liked to do stuff with her little brother. They would build with blocks and race toy cars, and dig in the mud for worms."

"Missy likes mud!" The toddler clapped her approval.

"Mommy doesn't like mud on the floor, though."

"Yeah." Claire grinned. She heard the front door open and close, and Justin returned. Since she'd started the story, she figured it would be best to finish it, even though Marie had only asked her to entertain them until Justin could take over again. "The queen didn't really like mud on the floor, either. She would make the princess and the prince mop the floor when they tracked too much inside. They didn't really like doing it. They did their chores anyway.

"They had a big yard, but the king didn't like grass very much, so they had lots of flowers and trees and bushes. Even though it was in the suburbs, they had a horse in the backyard. The king would ride it around when he surveyed his subjects and land and stuff. The queen rode in a chariot instead, and she went every day to do the business stuff because the king wasn't very good at any of that. While they were out on the weekdays, a..." She struggled for a few moments to find a good word to use for Stewy, their nanny. Funny how she couldn't remember his last name, just that it started like her own and sounded Italian. "A jester watched the prince and princess. Like a babysitter, kinda.

"Anyway, the princess. She had a bunch of friends at school, and sometimes she would go to a sleepover at one of their houses. It was fun to do something different and weird. Sometimes, they would all come to her house too. So everybody shared, and it was all fair. One day, the prince got sick, really bad, so he had to go to the doctor. Since it would be early in the morning on a Saturday, and the jester had the day off, the queen decided to send the princess on a sleepover with one of her friends. She thought that was awesome, because hospitals are icky, and Alicia was her best friend ever.

"So the princess went to Alicia's house and they had a really good time. They stayed up late and slept in, and Alicia's mom let them have ice cream on their waffles for breakfast. With strawberries." If she closed her eyes, sometimes she could still taste the berries. They'd come from the farmer's market downtown, and she'd never had better, juicier, sweeter, or fresher ones. "It was the best sleepover ever. The princess had to go home, though.

"Alicia's mom didn't think to call first to see if they'd come home from the hospital yet. They all got into the car and drove over to find—" Claire took a deep breath. "The king's house had burned down to the ground overnight. It happened before the king and queen and prince left." In that moment, she realized Lisa and Missy were just little kids who didn't need to hear this sort of story. They probably couldn't even understand it. She needed to find a way to make it fit a standard princess narrative.

"So the princess was all alone then. But the queen had given her a special present when she was very young, so young she couldn't remember it, a locket just like this one." She pulled the necklace out of her shirt and let them see it. The heart-shaped pendant held nothing, though it was large enough to encase a pocketwatch. Silver streaks marred the golden filigree of the front, caused by her thumb and fingers rubbing it over and over since the fire. "When she got it, she promised to take care of it and never lose it. Now she had to learn to keep that promise on her own."

"Girls, dinner is ready."

Claire heaved a sigh of relief, thankful for Marie's timing, because she wasn't sure where to take it from there. After helping Missy to the floor, she stood up and saw both Marie and Justin looking at her. They'd been listening. She tucked the locket safely under her shirt and dropped her gaze the floor, not wanting to see what they thought of her now.

She shuffled to the table and sat down in the chair Marie gestured for her to take. Missy sat on Justin's lap. They only had four chairs, and she'd taken one, forcing them to accommodate her. "I'm sorry," she told Marie. "I didn't mean—"

"It's alright." Justin let Missy feed herself from a small bowl while spearing his own food with a fork. "When you've got a story inside you, sometimes it needs to come out, no matter what you intended. I'm glad to know, at least, that I didn't aid and abet a runaway. Not a real one, anyway. I'm guessing you're in a group home right now?"

Looking back down at her hands in her lap, Claire nodded.

"I can take you to school in the morning."

"I got suspended for tomorrow," she murmured, "so that's not necessary. I can walk to the nearest bus stop. I've got a pass."

"Don't be silly." Marie patted her shoulder. "He can take you on Friday instead."

"What'd you get suspended for?"

"I beat up a guy who said some stuff."

"Huh."

She couldn't tell what that meant, so she raised her eyes to find him not watching her at all. "Are you going to call the cops?"

"No." Justin cracked a smile. "You asked me about a name earlier, Mark Terdan. How did you know him?"

Claire gulped. "That was my dad."

"So he died six years ago, in that fire."

She held her breath and thought her heart stopped beating. "Yes."

"Then I apologize for not being more forthcoming earlier. I've got the same job he did, and I even met him a few times."

She blinked at him and sucked in a breath. Then she blinked some more, utterly confused. "What?"

He grinned. "I'm gonna guess he didn't really talk about it to you and your brother much. My girls are aware I'm a Spirit Knight, though. Same as your dad was."

"Spirit—what? What are you talking about?" In a few short statements, Justin had gone from an eccentric but decent person to a lunatic. Claire stared, so confused she didn't know what to think about anything. "My dad was a park ranger."

Justin chuckled. "Yeah, well, in a way, that's part of what the job is. I heard you say he kept a horse in the backyard. You do know that a backyard isn't the kind of place you usually keep a horse, right? Not one in a city, anyway."

Claire opened her mouth to protest, then shut it. Visits from the police and animal control came to mind. The neighbors had complained. Some of her friends' mothers had made comments. Her brow furrowed. "I don't understand."

"Daddy protects us all from bad things that make animals go weird." Lisa beamed at her father.

"Wait, what?" Claire's eyes flicked from Missy to Justin. As much as she thought him nuts, if he could explain everything that had happened earlier, she'd listen. "There are bad things that make animals go weird?"

Justin nodded. "It's kind of complicated. Why? Do you know a young man who's having trouble with being chased by animals for no apparent reason?"

"No. It's me. Dogs and cats and birds all chased me down this afternoon." She lifted her leg to show him the bandages. "That's where I got all these scratches and bites. Nothing like that has ever happened to me before. I thought—I don't know what I thought. That they all got a memo about how I shouldn't be cutting school, I guess."

For what seemed to be several long seconds, Justin stared at her. His face slowly slid into a frown. "They don't usually attack at first, just chase. You must have something in your possession." After a pause, he added, "Girls can't be Knights."

Affronted and confused at the same time, she raised an eyebrow. "Why not?"

"It just never happens. Knights are always men. When you're done eating, we'll go outside and I'll see if I can figure out what it might be."

His words sounded final to Claire, and she turned back to her meal, wondering if she would've been better off staying in the office for the rest of the day.

CHAPTER 6

JUSTIN

Justin draped his cloak over his shoulders and stepped into his rubber boots again. He handed Marie's long purple coat to Claire so she wouldn't freeze in the crisp evening air, then watched her trudge outside with her head down. He hoped he could fix at least one of her problems. A Knight's daughter deserved more peace than she'd had. She also deserved help from the Knights, because he doubted that fire had been an accident. As he recalled, Avery, who managed to be both a Knight and keep his job as a Portland cop, had promised to look into it.

He considered forcing her into the woods until he checked her shoes. Her feet would go numb in this chill halfway to his sycamore. Instead, he took her to the wood-chopping clearing and had her sit on the stump. It should be good enough for this.

Tariel stepped into sight. "Have we decided to chop her up for firewood?"

"No, we've got enough to get through the winter already. Turns out she's got something on her that's attracting ur-phasms."

Claire squinted up at him with a sulky scowl. "Are you talking to the *horse*?"

Justin grinned. "Yes. She's a sprite. More or less, she's a dead person stuck in a horse."

Tariel snorted. "I love it when you talk dumb."

"And a pain in my ass. Every Knight has one, though they're not all horses."

"Are you saying...Kupiri was a dead person stuck in a horse?"

Justin moved to Tariel's side and rubbed her nose. No matter how annoying she got, he appreciated the several times she'd saved his life. "Yes. This isn't really why we're here, though."

"Why *are* we here?" Claire looked around. "Outside, I mean. You said everybody knows everything about your Spirit Knight stuff, so why can't we talk inside? It's freezing out here."

"Because we need to do more than talk, and it's best if Tariel helps me do the other part. Besides, just because my daughters know what I do, that doesn't mean I want them exposed to the actual work."

She sighed and rubbed her face with both hands. "Well, get on with it, then. Am I gonna live?"

Of course the teenage girl he'd rescued turned out to be sarcastic with a heaping helping of grumpy on top. He rolled his eyes and reminded himself sternly that she had cause to feel that way and he understood it. When he was her age, he'd been in his umpteenth foster home. It had made him a giant, cranky pain in the ass too.

Setting all that aside, he closed his eyes and took a deep breath, preparing to do something he'd only ever heard described before. Getting into the Palace happened by instinct. This stuff took effort. He raised his hand and focused on Claire, feeling Tariel's presence as an anchor. According to Kurt, he had to think really hard about the person he wanted to scan for Palace influence. Once he managed to tune his aura to hers, he'd be able to see...something. Assuming Kurt hadn't been speaking in code or yanking his chain.

Justin thought about the darkness of Claire's hair and the striped socks she still wore despite having been given a fresh pair of Marie's white ones. She clung to one of Missy's dolls, a patched and well-loved reminder of his own late grandmother.

She shifted on the stump, rolling her shoulders uncomfortably. "You're creeping me out."

He snorted. With a small shake of his head, he forced himself to focus. Then he saw it. A faint blue outline shimmered around her entire body and a bright white light gleamed over her heart. "Do you see what I'm seeing?"

Tariel bobbed her head. "Yes, and it's strange."

"'Strange' is kind of an understatement."

"I'm trying to protect your delicate male ego."

"That's a first."

Claire stomped to her feet. "Stop talking about me like I'm not here."

"I'm not," Justin said. "I'm just having a conversation with someone who only speaks Swahili about something only a dragon would understand."

Tariel whinnied a burst of laughter.

"This is serious, Tariel. She can't be a Knight. It's not possible."

Claire blinked, her petulance draining away. "Whoa. Wait. What?"

Tariel tossed her head and shoved him aside. "Denying what you can see doesn't make it less real. Suck it up. Accept and move on." She walked away twitching her tail.

According to every Knight he'd spoken to, only men had ever been Knights, and only men could ever be Knights. The order had records going back two millennia that clearly showed Knights had only ever been male. Kurt had told him that the most likely explanation was a gene on the Y chromosome that triggered a change between the ages of sixteen and eighteen.

Here stood the first female Knight, ever, and fate had chosen him to be her mentor. The responsibility of an apprentice crashed down onto his shoulders. While he'd known it would happen eventually, he'd hoped for another decade or two. That seemed to be a theme in his life. From the moment he'd lost his mother as a boy, life had rushed to shove as many duties as it could into his path.

"She's right." He watched his soulbound partner disappear behind the farmhouse. With a sigh, he turned to Claire. "You're going to be a Knight. No matter how impossible it is, it's happening."

"So...what's that mean?"

He crushed down a stab of jealousy. When it first happened to him, he'd had no idea what was going on. Claire would know and expect it all. "At some point in the near future, you're going to be drawn into a place we call 'the Palace.' No one really knows exactly where it is. You'll get pulled into it and find yourself in an empty bedroom with shelves on the walls, and your own personal bathroom. It's part of the dormitory wing—"

"I'm going to get my own room in a palace?" She gazed at him eagerly for the first time and hopped to her feet. "Let's go! Take me there now, I want to see that. I can sleep there instead of that stupid foster home."

"I can't." He sighed, because he understood. At her age, he'd felt the same. "A Knight can only take himself there. Herself. We don't open a doorway anyone can walk through, we transport ourselves there somehow. I'm not really clear on the nuts and bolts of how it works. I don't think anyone is."

"Okay." Her bright smile faltered. "You can teach me, then. Right?"

"No. Sorry." Seeing her deflate like this tugged at his heart. His girls did that sometimes when he had to leave. "It'll happen when it's time for it to happen. Until then, you just have to wait. Once it does happen, I can teach you other things, and you'll be able to get there on your own whenever you want. So it's still something to look forward to."

"I guess." She pinched a piece of the faded yellow yarn that served as hair for the doll and rolled it between her finger and thumb.

In her place, he thought he'd be wondering if this crazy guy might be lying to manipulate him, or testing him for some reason. He tried to think of some way to help her feel better about all of this, and came up blank. She'd have to wait, whether she liked it or not. In the meantime, he could give her a safe haven. Marie's father had done that for him.

"We can talk about it more later. For now, do you know how to fight? That's the most important skill to work on at the beginning. You can't be a Knight and not know how to fight."

Claire shrugged. She'd gone into a sulk, and he didn't know her well enough yet to guess at what might rouse her from it. Marie might have some ideas; she'd been a teenage girl up until a few years ago.

He stuck his thumbs into his back pockets. "Sounds like a no, but we don't have to fix that now. Think about what kind of fighting you want to learn, and I'll figure out a way for you to learn it. I'm kind of a traditional 'punching' and 'sword-swinging' guy, but there are Knights who do all kinds of martial arts, and use guns, bows, even spears and staves. You should go with whatever works for you."

Rubbing one arm, she looked down and her hair fell forward to obscure her face. "My dad used a sword."

"Yeah. I can teach you that, if you want. It's not too hard to pick up if you're willing to practice. You might do better with smaller blades, though. They're lighter, and you don't have a lot of muscle tone yet."

He had a feeling he could learn to hate teenage girl shrugs. "I guess."

"Okay, then. We'll start that tomorrow. For now, we need to find you a place to sleep. Marie's parents have a spare room, but I'm not sure it's wise to put you that far away when you could get sucked into the Palace at any moment. Do you mind sleeping on our couch?"

"I guess not."

Though he'd never been much of a praying man, and didn't strictly believe in God at this point, Justin sent up a prayer that neither Lisa nor Missy would turn out like this. Dealing with it once in his life would be plenty.

CHAPTER 7

CLAIRE

Claire settled on the couch with a blanket and pillow, amazed by how Justin doted on his girls, helping out with their baths and bedtimes. Her dad sometimes had handled that when Mom didn't make it home in time, but they never did it together. She almost wanted to hate Missy and Lisa for how lucky they were without knowing it, except Missy had given her the doll she still clutched.

She closed her eyes to try to sleep. Her mind refused to let her, churning over the day. She wondered what other secrets her parents had taken to their deaths that would come back to bite her in the butt. Mom had told her that the locket had been a present for her third birthday, something they got to cheer her up when she'd been very sick. Everything else but the few belongings she'd taken to Alicia's house that night had been lost in the fire, making it the only thing she had left of her parents besides faded memories.

Her father had been a Knight. Justin hadn't explained what they did, or why they even called themselves that. The fact she'd need to learn to fight with a weapon bothered her, though, because that meant things existed that needed to be fought with weapons. No matter what their actual purpose, a group of people usually only called themselves "knights" if they protected something or fought in some kind of war. Would she be expected to kill people? The thought made her cringe.

A vast gulf sat between beating someone up and killing them. She didn't want to imagine what Brian's parents would have to live through if she'd beaten him to death instead of just knocking him to the ground. The thought gave her flashes of the charred husk she'd seen when Alicia's mom took her home the next morning.

Alicia's mom sucked in her breath as soon as they turned down Claire's street, and the car rolled slowly to the mass of emergency vehicles blocking the way, lights flashing. Her neighbors loitered on the edges in sweatpants and robes, clumped together in chattering groups. Claire stared out the window, not comprehending any of it, not even when she realized that gaping space should be filled with her house.

The car stopped and a police officer approached the window. Alicia's mom rolled it down and cut him off as he started to tell her to turn around.

"Their daughter," she whispered, "she's in the car. She was at our house last night."

The cop blinked and turned to meet Claire's bewildered stare. He reached back to open the door her nose was pressed against. "We'll take care of her, ma'am. Thank you for bringing her back."

"I had no idea. Are they okay?"

"I'm sorry, ma'am. The parents and the boy were killed in the fire. We thought we just hadn't found her yet."

"I can take her home and take care of her until you can find a place for her."

"No, ma'am, I can't let you do that. We have to take her downtown." he opened the door, and Claire watched two men carry a black bag to a van. She still didn't understand yet. Not until she walked around the ambulance and saw the one blackened beam still standing, surrounded by more charred debris and the now-barren garden.

"There was a horse back here," someone shouted. "It's dead too!"

Hot tears slid down Claire's face and she knew she would never be able to kill another human being. Or anything else, for that matter, other than icky bugs. Defend herself, yes. She'd always do that, but with her fists and her knees—not a sword, not a dagger, not even a pair of scissors or a screwdriver. No one deserved to come home to something like that, or to never have someone come home to them.

She slipped into sleep unwillingly, surrendering to nightmares of fire and burning. A flaming hand tried to take the locket from her, and she held on to the chain until her flesh blistered and fell away. When she woke, she grabbed the locket, desperate to make sure she still had it. As she'd done many times during those first few weeks after the fire, she rubbed the warm metal on her cheek. She imagined it to be her mother's hand, offering what comfort she could.

A hand on her hair made her jump, and she saw a dark figure

outlined by a dim bulb that hung over the sink. The light flared around the figure's head in a halo. "I'm sorry," Marie whispered. "I heard you gasp and saw you move and thought you might be having a nightmare."

Claire took a deep breath and rolled onto her back, willing her heart to slow its frantic beating. "Yeah, sort of." She rubbed her eyes and looked around, seeing no one else. Lowering her voice to a whisper, she asked, "Do you want some help with breakfast?"

"No, go ahead and tie up the bathroom if you need to. Justin won't be up until the girls are, and that should be at least an hour." She stepped away, turning to the kitchen and the matter of food.

Claire rolled off the couch and disappeared into the bathroom, determined to take as little time as possible. She stripped and showered in tepid water, then realized she didn't have any clean clothes to change into. If only she'd stopped to grab her backpack before fleeing school—she always carried extra underwear in it. Or better yet, she could have picked up her emergency overnight bag. Either would have involved actually being able to remember her locker combination when she was that angry, which might have kept her standing there long enough to simmer down and go back to the office.

She could have gone back. She still could go back. At the group home, she could count on staying safe where no one cared about her. Here, it sounded like she had a dangerous job ahead of her, but Justin and Marie —however loony they might be—would watch over her. The choice confused her. Maybe she'd figure it out today, while Justin worked on whatever training he had planned for her.

Wrapped in a towel, she peeked her head out of the door, only to come face-to-face with a shirtless Justin rubbing his eyes, yawning, and reaching out to push the door open. She cleared her throat, trying to avoid staring at his chiseled six-pack abs, tight pecs, and thick biceps visible in the soft glow of the blue nightlight in the hall.

"Oh. Morning." He stood aside to let her pass.

Judging him to not be awake enough to leer at her, she grabbed her dirty clothes and ducked out. When she saw Marie in the kitchen, she hesitated to ask for anything. Clothing, however, seemed kind of important. "Um, can I—"

"Oh, you need fresh clothes. Sorry, I should've thought of that. Just a minute." Marie stopped making breakfast to hurry away.

If that woman apologized to her one more time for something no one should apologize for, she would...something. No real person behaved that way. Marie was too nice. That probably explained how she'd wound up with Justin, who was also too nice. These people couldn't actually be real. Heroic knights always had fatal flaws, like being a jerk, or stupidity, or serial infidelity.

Claire heard voices murmuring in the hallway, then the unmistakable smack of a quick kiss. Marie bustled back into the room, tossing clothes on the arm of the couch on her way to the kitchen. In the small pile, Claire found panties more red and racy than she expected Marie to have, a bra bigger than she could fill, and a plain T-shirt and sweatpants.

"I washed your socks and they dried overnight, but one's ripped. If you want them anyway, they're right here. Your shirt is still damp."

"Thanks." Claire pulled everything on except the bra, choosing to stick with her own. Looking down at herself, she felt frumpy, but that beat dead any day of the week. She grabbed her socks and yanked them on, not caring about the small rip. It served as a badge and a battle scar. All her scrapes and cuts had been cleaned and re-wrapped, and she felt confident they would heal well enough.

The doll sat on the couch beside her, staring up with its fixed smile. As much as she wanted to carry it around to ward off the crazy animals, she knew that would never work. Besides, she had a feeling Missy would have second thoughts about giving it up. With a sigh, she settled it in the corner of the couch and left it there.

When she walked into the kitchen, as ready for the day as she felt likely to get, Marie pressed her into service pouring and flipping pancakes. Justin emerged fully dressed a little while later, and the two girls filled the space with noise and bouncing and joy soon after. They still only had four chairs, and Missy seemed delighted by the problem forcing her to sit on her father's lap again.

"I'm going to be out all day with Claire today," Justin announced to the table after swallowing his last bite. "We've got things that need doing, and they'll take until dark. That means you two are going to have dinner with Grandma and Grandpa, and I expect to hear you haven't given them any trouble. Lisa, I know I can count on you to get ready for the bus on time on your own today."

"Yes, Daddy!" Lisa beamed and held up a forkful of pancake proudly. "I will. I'll be ready early, even, and walk myself to the bus stop."

"Let Grandpa Jack walk you up there, Sprout. Don't go alone."

"Yes, Daddy. I'll go tell him after breakfast."

"Good plan." He kissed the top of Missy's head and stood up, then stationed her in his chair. "Claire, be ready to go in about ten minutes." Apparently in a hurry to go, he chugged his orange juice as he strode to the back of the house.

"Yes, sir," Claire said with a mock salute, then she shoveled food into her mouth and choked it down. She hopped up, unwilling to discover what he'd be like if she kept him waiting, and took both his plate and her own to the sink.

"Feel free to borrow a coat or sweater from the mud room on your way out," Marie said.

Ten minutes later, she stood outside the front door in a green sweater and her own shoes. Lisa darted past her in genuine wooden clogs with Justin right behind her, shooing her along. He had his chainmail and pauldrons on again, along with the cloak, and worked to buckle his sword belt as the door smacked shut behind him.

He led the way to the wood-chopping clearing. "I've got a hunch I want to check on, so we'll be in Portland most of the day. I wouldn't take you along for that, but at some point, we do need to stop by your foster home and let them know you're not dead or kidnapped. It would be a huge waste of time to go and come back twice when I can do it just once. Besides, it won't hurt you to get an idea of what the job's like."

"Uh. Yay? How are you going to convince my foster parents not to report anything to the cops?"

"I'll be persuasive."

She grinned at his back. Then she stopped and blinked, because the horse stepped into view, already wearing its saddle and bridle. "Did you leave those on Tariel, or can she put her stuff on herself?"

"There's a bunch of birds and squirrels that do it for us."

"And they all swoop in and clean the house while Marie sings, right?"

"Yep. Fridays are kind of crazy." With a straight face, he stuck his foot in the stirrup and hauled himself into the saddle, then reached down to help her up. "Fortunately, they're nice enough to crap outside."

"You're joking right?" She grabbed his hand, stepped on his boot, and jumped. Climbing up seemed smoother this time, taking less of his effort and using more of her own.

He chuckled. "Yes. Tariel can handle having the saddle on all night, so long as I don't do it all the time. When I realized we'd need to go out this morning anyway, I didn't bother to go out last night and remove it."

Somehow, this knowledge made her more comfortable. "Oh my gosh, I was starting to think Marie was Snow White."

"Nah." They trotted down the dirt drive and out onto the street. "I'm a Knight, not a prince. And I don't think I would have opened a casket to kiss her. That's just freakish."

He probably saw the irony of himself referring to something as "freakish." Claire shut her mouth and watched the scenery go by as Tariel sped up and took them deeper into wilderness. They plunged off the road and galloped through trees, where drops of morning dew splashed on her face. She had no idea why they'd come out here and lost herself in the rhythm of the ride.

Her father had taken her out on Kupiri for quick rides around the neighborhood, but he'd never raced through the woods with her. She looked back to see Justin watching the path ahead of them, and wondered if he ever took Marie out like this. Other ideas about what else they might do on Tariel's back popped into her head, making her blush. To make matters worse, she wondered if he'd ever do anything like that to her.

"Let me know if you need a break." His voice shattered her errant daydreams.

"Will do." Obviously, he had Marie, and they were perfect for each other. He was a perfect dad and a perfect gentleman and a perfect Knight and a perfect husband, and Marie was perfect too. She ought to just admire the example they set and be grateful for it.

CHAPTER 8

JUSTIN

The time spent riding around in the woods helped Justin center himself and gave him time to think. As much as he loved his family and had plenty of woods to jog through at home, sometimes a ride with Tariel cleared his head and made thinking a thousand times easier.

Ur-phasms had chosen to attack Claire, probably because she had the signs of a budding Knight. Until she found her way to the Palace, she'd be vulnerable and easy for them to find. They'd also be able to best her if she stopped long enough outside protected spaces. Without a weapon, she stood little chance of fending them off for long, and then they'd devour her essence, killing her and becoming corrupt ne-phasms.

Not on his watch.

The question he needed answered was whether they'd done it because they'd been ordered to, or because their master let them do whatever they wanted. To find out, he needed to grab one and ask it. He turned Tariel toward Portland, because he had a destination now. As she usually did, she sped up in response to his unvoiced wishes and new urgency.

They dove out of the woods and onto a road. Tariel's silver hooves clacked on the asphalt as she reached and exceeded the speed limit. The run took them to and across the I-205 bridge in the breakdown lane, and he covered Claire with his cloak again to keep her safe from flying debris. Tariel threw what Kurt called a force field around him by virtue of their bond, but he'd never thought to ask if it extended to a passenger.

Once off the bridge, he had Tariel leave the freeway. It slowed them down, but it also made them less conspicuous. For some reason, people stared more at a mounted knight traveling eighty miles an hour along the freeway than one trotting up city streets. Portland, go figure. He let Claire out from under the cloak.

"Where are we going?"

"Where you were attacked. What do you remember about the route you took?"

"I, uh, started at school. Grant High. Took a mostly straight line to where you found me."

"Tariel, let's start at the school." He pulled the reins to the left.

She shook her head and turned to the right. "You're an idiot. This way is faster."

He rolled his eyes. "Oh, fine. Go your way."

They trotted through the streets of east Portland, passing stone churches squatting beside modern buildings. He'd grown up in Vancouver, and every visit to this side of the river showed him something new. Today, he noticed a random silver sculpture in the middle of an intersection. Like all the other random sculptures scattered across the city, he had no idea how to interpret it.

They reached her high school, and he had Tariel walk the streets around the campus. They cut across the park attached to the side. "This is public ground, which, for reasons beyond me, is protected from ur-phasms. I'm guessing yesterday was the first time you'd wandered off from the usual places in a while?"

She took a few seconds to answer, then nodded. "Yeah, I guess so. I spend a lot of time at police stations, my social worker's office, my therapist's office, school, the bus, and whatever place I'm living in."

"You could've been throwing off the signs for a while, then. Where did you step off school grounds?"

Under her direction, Tariel took them to a break in the shrubs and trees, then onto the street. Claire pointed down the street. "That's where the dog was, and up there, that's where the cat flew out of nowhere."

Tariel avoided the house with the dog, which jumped up anyway and strained at its leash without barking. "She ran quite a long way to get to where we found her."

The observation—and the ur-phasm on the leash—made him hold the girl a little tighter. It sounded as though she'd had a rougher day than he'd realized. "Let's check that place with the cat. It's probably a stray." He noted the address with the dog because he'd have to come back and deal with it later. Right now, he needed information and didn't have time to apply the finesse needed to prevent a lawsuit from the owners of a beloved pet dog.

When they reached the spot, he let go and hopped down. "Stay up there," he told Claire. To Tariel, he said, "Anything happens, you get her to safety."

Tariel followed him as he checked the dumpster and white plaster wall of a convenience store. She snuffled the air and waved her head around. "It smells like a breeding ground."

The area stank of cat, and garbage lay strewn about. Lumps of stained cardboard probably housed mice and rats. Ur-phasms would have a field day here, finding hosts, devouring them, and riding their empty husks. "Yeah, that's what I'm getting here too." He stooped and brushed a mailed glove across the concrete, sweeping greasy fast food wrappers aside. "We need to catch one of them."

A feline scream made all three of them look up. As a cat-shaped ur-phasm flew through the air, Tariel side-stepped and prevented it from landing on Claire's head. Instead, the ur-phasm hit Justin's arm and hooked its claws into his armor. He let it hiss and gnaw ineffectually for a moment, then grabbed it around the neck and held it out. "Look at this, we got a live one."

The ur-phasm kept hissing and spitting as he walked up the street, trying to claw its way out of his grip. He ignored it until he reached a nearby church parking lot, which he jogged across to the corner where he thought the smallest number of passersby would see anything. Tariel had followed in his wake with Claire still on her back.

"Alright. Spill." He held the ur-phasm up and squeezed it.

Claire sucked in a breath. "You're not going to hurt it, are you?"

"We'll see."

The ur-phasm stopped struggling, its body going limp. "I hate you."

"No, really? I never would've guessed." He snorted. "Are you working for someone or on your own?"

"I'm just a free ur." It sounded helpless and pathetic—and completely fake.

He knew there was no such thing as an actual free ur-phasm. Playing dumb, though, might get him more information. "I'm not sure I believe you." He squeezed enough to make its eyes bug out.

"I swear, I swear! It's just me and a couple other urs here! The girl looks tasty, that's all, nothing else. She's full of sweet, sweet untapped energy, and it makes all of us drool just to look at her. Ter—tomorrow, uh...we're gonna—"

"Look," Justin said, "first it was just you, now it's you and your posse. I know you're lying to me, which means your life isn't worth a whole lot to you, and that being the case, I'm thinking pretty hard about letting my horse eat you."

The ur-phasm waggled its hind legs, trying to wriggle free. "There's really no Phasm around here."

"You're so full of crap," he said with disgust. In honesty, he had no idea if the thing told the truth or not. He, of course, had no intention of letting it go, since killing these things comprised at least half his job. Holding the mangy shell up, he gestured for Tariel to come forward. She paced to him, which made the ur-phasm freak out.

"N-no! Wait, okay, you got me." It squirmed and flailed, mad to get free. "It's shacked up someplace else. I don't know where, I swear."

"Too little, too late," Justin growled.

Tariel took this as a signal and lunged at his hand. She snapped her mouth around the ur-phasm's head and chomped down, punching through its neck. Justin flung the headless, bloody cat corpse away and Tariel spat the head out in a different direction. He turned to say something to Tariel and noticed Claire staring, her face pale, her eyes wide with shock, and her mouth hanging open.

"You just...she just... Its *head*—" She gasped for breath, and threw herself off the horse. In her haste, she landed on her butt. Scrambling to her feet, she held out a hand to ward him off, then turned and bolted.

"Claire!" He clambered onto Tariel's back. "Chase her down."

They caught up in seconds. Justin leaned down and scooped her up. She screamed and flailed while he hauled her across his lap. Tariel launched into a gallop, weaving between cars so fast she'd have to be stupid to jump down, even if he didn't have a grip on the waistband of her pants. The great beast would trample her by accident when she landed, or a car would run her over.

When they reached a park, he pulled Tariel to a stop and slid to the ground, taking Claire with him. Holding her close, her back against his chest, he tried to calm her down, yet she kept wailing. "It's okay, Claire. Listen to me!"

"Cop," Tariel grunted.

He looked up and had a good idea of how this must look: adult male in knight costume wrestles screaming teenage girl. "It's okay, officer. She's just having a panic attack."

After flashing him a look skeptical enough to blister paint, the cop bent to try to catch Claire's eye with a friendly, sympathetic smile. "Miss? Are you in any danger?"

Thankfully, she stopped screaming. She panted for a second, and he thought she might nod. "Lunatic," she breathed.

At this point, he shifted gears from "protect the girl" to "avoid getting arrested." Later, he'd let himself feel the sting of betrayal. "Claire," he said with a sigh. Letting her go, he held his hands up for the cop. "We hit a cat back there. She freaked out."

The cop flicked his eyes between them and settled his attention on her. "Is that your name, miss? Claire?"

CHAPTER 9

CLAIRE

"Yeah." She blinked and caught her breath. "Claire." How did she think the guy was perfect just a few hours ago? Justin had convinced her of his compassion and awesomeness by being sweet to his family and to her. When it came down to it, he was nothing like that.

"And are you alright?"

She pushed away from Justin and to the cop. "No, he's a freak! He killed that cat, just like that!"

The cop wrapped an arm around her. "It's okay, Claire, you're safe now."

"I'm not abducting her." Justin sounded reasonable and long-suffering. "Claire, what are you doing?"

She buried her face in the cop's shoulder and tried to block out their voices. "Leave me alone," she whined.

"Fine," he grunted. "You've got the gun, she's all yours." His chainmail jingled away, and Tariel's hooves clopped into the distance.

"It's safe now, Claire. He's gone." The officer pushed her away far enough to see her face. "Do you know him?"

"I thought I did." She sniffled and wiped her nose on Marie's sweater.

"Did he try to do anything inappropriate to you?"

She chewed on her thumbnail without meeting his eyes. "No. He's just a weirdo."

"Let's get you tucked in." He walked her to his squad car and settled her into the back seat. He climbed in behind the wheel and asked for her address. Once she'd told him, she sat back and watched the scenery go by, falling into mute shock by the time the cop car pulled up to her foster home. Numb, she did nothing while the foster mother—she forgot the woman's name—shouted at her about being out all night and getting suspended and fighting at school and dodging her social worker. When the woman finally ran out of things to yell about, Claire ghosted upstairs to the room she shared with three other girls the same age and rolled into her top bunk to stare at the ceiling.

Nothing that happened with Justin or Marie had been real. She'd slept in a shelter someplace and conjured them as a dream of how life could be. Tomorrow, she would go back to school, and no one would mess with her, because they knew now that she could beat the crap out of any of them. That fight had been worth it, even if she did get suspended. One day didn't matter. Nothing worth paying attention to happened on Thursdays anyway.

Her roommates asked questions, wanting to know if anyone had hurt her, if she got arrested, and a dozen other things. When she ignored them, they gave up and left her alone. She stared at the ceiling until dinnertime, convincing herself Justin didn't exist and her father hadn't been anything other than eccentric. After dinner, which she ate in silence and without interest, she went back up to bed and stared more.

Only a few minutes after she climbed into bed again, the door creaked open and shut. "Claire," a voice whispered. Dim light coming in through the window glinted off Drew's glasses when his head popped up next to her. "Are you awake?"

Had it been anyone else, she would have stayed silent. "Yeah."

"Can I come up?"

"I guess."

The bed creaked, groaned, and danced as he climbed the ladder at her feet. "Budge over." He crawled up the bed and pushed her until she rolled onto her side. Two years ago, they'd both gotten into trouble for doing this. Nothing had happened between them; they just both couldn't sleep and needed more warmth than their thin blankets could provide. He settled in behind her and held her close.

"Everyone was talking about you at school today," he murmured into her ear. "'Claire is a real badass. Don't mess with her. She'll kick your ass if you stare at hers for too long.' I mentioned you'd punched a teacher in the face at your old school. I think it scared some of them."

"Thanks, I think."

"What's wrong, Claire? What happened to you last night?"

"I don't want to talk about it." She breathed in his scent, a combination of soap, sweat, and toothpaste. "Tell me stuff will be okay."

"Stuff will be okay. You only have one and a half more years until you age out. I'll be out already by then, and we can get a place together. Just you and me. Some dinky apartment with cheap linoleum and a stove with only three burners working. Go to college. Work crappy jobs until we're done and have degrees."

It sounded nice, a fond dream to hope for. When she turned to smile at him, she discovered he'd taken off his glasses and tucked them into the collar of his shirt. She lay there, not quite face to face with the one person she felt she could trust, her eyes flicking back and forth between his. The skin between his brown freckles darkened and his cheek radiated heat.

"Claire, you're really pretty." He brushed her forehead, pushing some of her black hair aside.

She wanted him to kiss her. Not sure how to get him to ask or say what she wanted, she wriggled around to face him fully and had no idea what to do with her arms. Should she put this hand on his chest and the other one on his hip? Both on his chest? Wrap this one around herself and put the other one on his arm?

He seemed just as flustered. Both of them shifted, hands tentative and awkward. Finally, he touched her cheek and pressed his lips to hers, hesitant and light. The only kissing Claire had seen recently happened in movies, and she did what the actors did, making him follow suit. His mouth tasted minty.

The door opened to let in two girls chattering about something. Claire and Drew froze at the same time, and she willed her roommates not to look, not to notice, not to tell anyone. They talked about math homework, and Drew gulped when it sounded as though they were changing into their pajamas. He kept his eyes on her, showing her that he didn't care about them. His fear echoed her own. If this foster father caught them together, one of them would get locked in the basement, and then the system would make sure they got separated for good.

Just when Claire thought they'd never leave, both girls chattered their way out to the bathroom, not bothering to close the door on their way out. "Be careful," she whispered to Drew. He kissed her again, this time with a swift brush of his lips on hers, then he jumped down from her bunk and hurried to the door. After peeking out, he ran for it, headed up the hall to the room he shared with three other boys.

She hugged herself. Everything with Justin had been a fabrication, a lie. This was real. It felt good. Tomorrow, she and Drew would ride the bus together, and have gym class together, and meet out by the tennis courts at lunch. It would be a good day, a better one than the last two.

Chapter 10

Justin

Tariel plodded up the street with all the enthusiasm Lisa had for taking a bath: none. "You should have fought harder for her."

"Shut up." Justin clenched his jaw and wrenched the reins to the side, forcing the horse to take the cross street.

"Ow, quit it. You can't just let her go like that."

"I said shut up." He stewed, wanting to punch something.

"Pull your head out of your behind, Knight. Where are we going?"

Crossing his arms to restrain the urge to thump her between the ears, he grunted. "Take us home. She's safe enough with the cops for now."

"It's going to happen in the worst possible place."

"Yeah, and that's life. Stuff a cork in it and take us home. I need to think."

"Great. That means it'll be three days before we do anything else."

She flicked her ears when he scowled and launched into a gallop.

He'd stopped that ur-phasm from clawing her up any more than it already had, and yet she freaked out and told him to leave her alone. It reminded him of the first time he'd held Lisa and she wouldn't stop crying. The midwife had said that was normal, that babies cried for the first minute or so. Despite that, he'd felt helpless and weak, stupid and foolish. In that moment, he hadn't been able to think of anything he wanted more than the power to comfort the tiny bundle in his arms. Then Marie had solved it by waving her magic mommy wand. Somehow, he had a feeling she couldn't fix this so easily. He'd have to figure it out for himself.

The scenery rushed past as they streaked north faster than the traffic, matching the pace of dark clouds rolling in. They reached the farm, and he took Tariel to pull her saddle and bridle off, then brushed her down. For once, she kept quiet, sensing the sourness of his mood. When he finished, she gave him a long, slow blink and settled in her stable, where she'd be warm and dry through the incoming storm.

Outside, the clouds opened up and dumped on him. He slogged through the mud in the sudden downpour, getting spattered and soaked. The axe caught his eye. He tugged his mailed gloves back on, grabbed the axe, and set up a log on the old stump in the clearing. Ignoring the rain pelting down on him, he swung the axe and wedged it into the middle of the log, cracking it in half. He wrenched the two halves apart and dropped one while setting the other up. Another swing split the half into quarters.

Three logs later, his mind had settled, as it always did. He stacked up the new firewood in the lean-to behind the farmhouse to dry and leaned the axe against the wall. In the cottage's mud room, he peeled soaked boots, socks, and gloves off, and hung his cloak up. Since the socks were wet enough to drip, he left them behind and went inside.

"Daddy!" Missy ran and jumped into his arms, convinced he would catch her.

He lifted her up and kissed her forehead, then set her back down. "Not now, Pumpkin. Go play with Mommy." Thank goodness Lisa would still be at kindergarten now.

"What's wrong?" Marie remained sitting on the floor where she'd been playing with the toddler. Her brow knit with concern.

She had enough to worry about and deal with. He mustered a smile and waved her off as he headed for the bedroom. "Nothing. Just a—" He sighed. "It's nothing."

"I thought you'd be longer. Where's Claire?"

"It's complicated." In the bedroom, into which he did not now flee, he dismissed the enchantment holding the pauldrons to his chainmail and settled them on their stand. With another wave of his hand, the chain shirt released its tight grip on his torso and arms, and he wriggled out of it.

"Complicated like you're having pervy old man thoughts about a teenage girl, complicated like you can't stand her because she's a teenage girl, or complicated like you did something stupid?" Marie stood in the doorway, leaning against the frame with her arms crossed and her mouth drawn down in an annoyed frown.

"I'm *not* a pervy old man," he grumbled with his back to her, yanking his shirt off. "My dad is a pervy old man, not me."

She huffed out a half-laugh. "You did something stupid, didn't you."

Glancing back, he caught her smirking at him and scowled. "It was *not* stupid." He crossed his arms over his bare chest and glared out the window. With the ratty old brown curtains drawn aside this morning to let the sunshine in, he had a great view of the already lessening storm. "I did what I had to do."

Marie came up behind him and wrapped her arms around him. Her head settled on his shoulder, and she brushed her cheek against him. "You did what you *thought* you had to do. It had an unintended side effect, right?"

He sighed, always soothed by her touch. "Something like that."

"What happened?"

"An ur-phasm tried to kill her. I killed it and she freaked out."

She kissed his shoulder. "I have a feeling you're leaving some parts out."

He frowned, realizing he could have handled that situation better. "I questioned it first. Tariel bit its head off."

Squeezing him around the middle, Marie stayed quiet.

"It had a cat shell. She saw me offer it a chance to live, then my horse killed it, making me the Mighty Kitten Slayer." Letting his arms relax and fall to his sides, he shook his head. "You're right, I did something stupid."

"I love you, Jay."

He lifted a hand to cover his face. "That was the dumbest thing I've done in a week."

"Give yourself a little credit. It's been at least a month since you did anything *that* dumb."

"I'm not ever going to live down that mud thing, am I?"

She stepped around until she stood in front of him and tugged his arm down, then smiled up at him. "Missy is scarred for life, I'm sure." She brushed imaginary lint off his arm. "I know you always do the best you can with what's in front of you." She cupped his face in both hands. "And I don't regret choosing to marry you over the other options I had. I wouldn't trade Lisa or Missy for the world, or you. I wish some things could be different, but I don't have any regrets."

"I don't deserve you." He settled his hands on her hips and pulled her closer. Her lips mesmerized him and her warmth reminded him what he fought for.

She grinned. "No, you really don't."

Their kiss had to end when Missy clapped and squealed with joy from the doorway. She ran in and thumped into his leg, then wrapped her pudgy little arms around it and squeezed. "Daddy, I want hugs and kisses too!"

"Oh, really?" He let go of Marie to grab the girl and swung her up so she could hug his neck. "Maybe we should sit on the couch and read a book together."

Marie hooked a finger through one of his belt loops. "What about Claire?"

He carried Missy and dragged Marie into the family room. "She'll be fine for a day or two. I'll let her calm down and think, and go find her this weekend. Speaking of this weekend, maybe we should have a sleepover at Grandma and Grandpa's."

"Yay!" Missy pressed her chubby little face to his and giggled. "I want a Grandpa Jack story!"

"We'll get one for you tomorrow." Justin smiled, grateful for a sweet little girl who could banish his worries with her laughter.

CHAPTER 11

CLAIRE

"Claire, you need to go to the office." Ms. Caper hung up the classroom phone and pointed at the door.

"What? Why? I didn't *do* anything." Sniggers throughout the room made her scowl.

"I don't know. Class is almost over. Take your things and go."

Grumbling under her breath about stupid interruptions and being singled out, Claire slung her notebook and English book into her backpack, grabbed it, and stormed out of the room. For one wild moment, she thought about running for it again. The animals attacking her had been a weird anomaly, and the fantasy her mind had constructed of Justin and Marie and the two girls had given her something to retreat to when things got bad.

She wanted to see Drew again at lunch more than she wanted to run away. When she reached the office, a man in a tan suit stood chatting with the elderly secretary and Mr. Gary. All three turned to look at her.

"You're not in trouble, Claire." Mr. Gary beckoned her closer. "Detective Avery just wants to talk to you."

The middle-aged man in the unremarkable suit offered his hand to her, and she took it, finding him attractive for some reason. The attraction had nothing to do with romance; it felt like kinship, brotherhood, trust. He smiled at her, and, despite having no reason to, she smiled in return.

"Hi, Claire. I just want to ask you a few questions. Do you want Mr. Gary to be present?"

"She's a minor, Detective, I'm afraid that's required by law when a guardian can't be here. There's also the small matter of your conflict of interest here."

Claire's head turned from one man to the other, and she frowned at the principal. "Can you just leave the door open and sit out here?" She had no idea why it mattered, but somehow knew Mr. Gary's presence would make the experience less pleasant.

"I can get the school counselor. That would be more proper." Mr. Gary waved a hand to the secretary.

"It's alright," Detective Avery said. "This won't take that long."

Mr. Gary echoed Claire's frown. "That's not really..."

"It'll be fine. I've already told you it's not about Brian." Detective Avery put his arm around her shoulders and guided her inside the principal's office. He left the door open, as she suggested, and nudged her into one of the chairs. She sat obediently and watched him. "So, Claire." He sat in Mr. Gary's chair.

"Yes, Detective?" She sat up straight, eager to help him.

He smiled at her again, and she beamed. "According to a police report, you were found yesterday in the company of this gentleman." He pulled a picture out of the inside pocket of his suit jacket and set it in front of Claire. The image showed Justin from a distance, looking to the side with his face in focus. She recognized his short black hair, the shape of his shoulders, and, of course, the brilliant green cloak.

It struck her that his cloak had been in such good condition when everything else in his life, from his work boots to his couch to the towels in the bathroom, seemed faded and worn and frayed. The cloak could have been made yesterday and resisted the mud he tromped through around his house.

Avery continued. "The officer noted you were, quote, screaming and hysterical, end quote. This man is also noted as admitting to killing a cat, though he claimed it to be accidental."

Claire's smile faltered and she slunk into a slouch. None of that had really happened. Her sanity depended on all of it being a weird fabrication designed to shield her from whatever other awful thing had happened Wednesday night.

When she remained silent, Avery put a hand over Justin's picture and leaned in. "Claire, I'm really not here about you beating my son up. You were suspended, and I'm sure that losing your parents has made things hard for you. The only thing you really damaged was his ego and pride, and in all fairness, he probably deserved that."

"What?" She squinted at him, confused.

Avery blinked and sat back. "Did you not know Brian's last name?"

"Uh, no. I just transferred here on Monday."

"Then what's the matter? You look like you think you're in

trouble."

She reached out and touched the picture with one finger. If all that had really happened, then she freaked out because the nicest person she'd met since her family died had killed a cat that had clawed and bit her. From the way it had launched itself at her yesterday, it must have intended to kill her.

"I...don't know." She brushed her fingertips across the image. None of this made any sense. She wanted to believe in the possibility of people like Justin and Marie existing. Time and time again, she'd been shown the world didn't work that way, but she still *wanted* to believe.

"Do you know his name?"

"Justin."

"And his family name?"

"I'm not sure."

"Claire."

She looked up and found him giving her a polite yet skeptical smile. "I really don't know. Did he do something wrong?"

"He stole a priceless piece from the Oregon Historical Society, and he's wanted for questioning in connection to another theft in Salem, in addition to a few counts of fleeing the scene and half a dozen other minor charges." Avery drummed his fingers on the desk in the silence. "How did you meet him?"

She shrugged and dropped her eyes to her lap. "Just ran into him. Accident and all."

"I see. Did you spend the night with him on Wednesday?"

"Yeah." Her nose itched, so she rubbed it.

Avery's fingers beat on the desk three more times, then he stood up in a sharp, decisive motion. "I'm taking you into protective custody, Claire."

Stunned, she blinked and stared at him. "What? Why?"

"I'm concerned about your safety, especially when I can now add child endangerment, contributing to the delinquency of a minor, and statutory rape to the charges against him." He grabbed her arm and hauled her to her feet with strength she didn't expect, then hustled her out of the office. "Let's keep that quiet, Mr. Gary," he said as he dragged her past him.

"No, wait. Nothing like that happened! He's married with little kids and was really nice." She struggled against his grip to no avail. "I told him I got suspended, so he just gave me a place to stay!"

Avery shoved her out the door and flashed a sad smile at the secretary, then hauled her to his unremarkable sedan. He yanked the rear passenger door open and threw her inside. Before she recovered from the toss, he grabbed her hands and slapped a pair of handcuffs on her. "Settle down or I'll *make* you settle down," he growled.

Claire froze, terrified of this guy. How did she have thought for even a moment that she could trust him? "Is this about Brian?"

"No, Claire, it's not. But I will admit that incident does make this all the sweeter." He threw the door shut.

While he walked around the car, she tossed herself at the door and found the handle didn't work. The bastard must have engaged the child-safety locks. To her surprise, the rear seat belt snapped down of its own accord and buckled itself, holding her in the seat. She lunged against it, and it didn't give her any slack.

Avery slid into the driver's seat and the engine purred to life. "Relax, Claire." He twisted around to watch her while backing the car out of its parking space. "The more you struggle, the worse it'll be for you."

"What are you? What is this thing?"

He smiled, full of dark amusement. "You really are just a child."

She had no idea how to interpret that and watched in mute horror as the car sped down the city streets without Avery's hands on the wheel, taking her away from the one place Justin might be able to find her. "Where are we going?"

"Downtown. You'll be processed and held until such time as you decide to answer all my questions."

She gulped. Was the car his version of Tariel? If he was a Knight, though, why was he treating her this way? "You don't have to do all that. I'll answer whatever questions you wanna ask. I still don't know Justin's last name, though. I didn't ask, and he didn't tell me."

Avery's brown eyes, which had seemed so friendly and welcoming at first, gave her a flat, cold stare in the rearview mirror. "Does he know your last name?"

Claire frowned and let her eyes settle on the back of Avery's seat. She wanted him to believe that she needed to think about the question. If she spent enough time acting helpful and pretending to try her best, he might come to the wrong conclusions about her. From what Justin had said, she expected the Knights to welcome her into the group. That this guy didn't made her think she needed to keep him guessing. "I don't know. Maybe. All I can say for sure is he knows where I go to school."

"You said you stayed at his house. Where is it?"

If she gave him nothing, he'd probably assume she was lying. She'd have to be vague. Hopefully, she could make her answer vague enough, because she had to keep this creep from going after Marie and the girls.

"Um, north? I don't really know. I was kind of freaking out when he picked me up and not really paying attention when we came back. I guess I remember going across a bridge."

"I see," he grumbled. "What did his house look like? The yard?"

"Um." She shrugged. "A house? With trees? I dunno, I mostly saw the inside, not the outside. Small, I guess. I really wasn't there very long."

He harrumphed and turned his back on her as the car maneuvered itself through the streets. It pulled into a parking garage and descended into its fluorescent bowels. A sign informed her they'd arrived at a police station.

"I answered all your questions," she protested.

"Yes, you did."

"Then why are we here?"

"Did you really think I'd just let you go?" He snorted as he settled the car into a parking space. "He's obviously connected to you. You'll be down here until he comes looking."

Sparks of panic jolted through her body. "You can't just keep me in jail for no reason."

"Sure I can. We do that all the time." He stepped out and yanked her door open, his arm moving in a flash to grab her before she could escape. Hauling her out of the car, he squeezed her arm so tight she thought he'd leave a bruise. "Make a fuss and you get to see what we do to people for resisting arrest." He pulled hard enough to make her stumble and dragged her to the nearest building entrance.

"What am I being arrested for?"

"Truancy."

She gaped up at him. "I was suspended!"

"Ah. Good point." After a brief pause, he said, "Fighting, then. Zero tolerance is harsh these days. Especially when a witness reported you had a knife."

"Nobody said that, you're just making stuff up!"

"It's a shame how you're turning out, Claire. Most kids do fine in the system here. You, though? Fighting, running away, using drugs, shoplifting..."

"What?"

They stepped into an elevator, and she struggled in his grip. He squeezed again, this time until she stopped with a whimper and watched the doors close. "Of course, all this will be cleared up as soon as I have Justin. Until then, your paperwork will be mysteriously difficult to locate."

"Wait. I, um." Claire imagined herself inside juvenile hall—or worse, shuffled into an adult prison "by accident"—and had no idea what to do.

Avery peered down his nose at her. "Well? You have something else to say? Spit it out."

She gulped.

The elevator doors opened. People, most in police uniforms, bustled about with folders, clipboards, or computer tablets. A female officer stepped into the elevator, giving Avery a polite nod. Avery tightened his grip again. Afraid he'd do worse things if she struggled, she stayed quiet. They stepped out on the next floor.

She searched faces as they walked down a hallway, wishing one would seem sympathetic. None did. Avery tossed her into a dingy little room with a metal table flanked by two metal chairs, where he clipped her handcuffs into a metal loop on one side of the table. It locked in somehow, ensuring she couldn't leave without dragging the table along. He slammed the door shut, leaving her there alone.

Scenarios flashed through her mind. One had Justin bursting in to rescue her. Another had Avery torturing her until she gave him Justin's address. Wilder ideas cropped up of him having an evil master or mistress somewhere. He'd rough her up. When that didn't work, he'd take her to this cartoonish supervillain and leave her there. When they finished doing whatever they wanted with her, he'd kill her and throw her body in the river.

Him being a cop confused her. Cops were supposed to uphold the laws, not throw people in jail for no reason. On top of that, she figured Knights would all be like Justin. Except Avery had told her, point-blank, that he would lie to keep her in jail for as long as he needed to. And she had no idea why. Fresh panic made her yank at her hands. Nothing happened, except for the cuffs scraping her wrists.

"I need to get out of here," she told the room. Twisting in a panic, she noticed the camera perched in one corner near the ceiling. "Let me out," she begged it. "I didn't do anything! He's crazy. Please let me out!" She pulled on the cuffs again. "I just want to go home, please let me go home." She reached for whatever words would help, and found none. "Please," she repeated, her eyes burning with tears.

The door flew open, and she flinched away from it. Though the cuffs prevented her from hiding all the way under the table, she ducked down and tried to use it as a shelter. "Don't hurt me," she whimpered into her arms.

Avery chuckled. "I didn't even do anything yet, Claire. Here's how this is going to go. You're going to tell me everything you know about

Justin. You will not leave this room until you do. That's it, end of story." He scraped a chair across the industrial-tile floor and draped his suit jacket over the back. "We can do this the easy way or the hard way, of course. I think you'd prefer the easy way, because I think you don't want to discover what the hard way is really like."

Her mouth went dry and her voice cracked when she tried to speak. His rumbling laughter sparked a fire in her belly. She popped her head up to glare over the table at him. "You can't just beat me up in here. There's a camera, and the other officers won't let you."

"Oh, Claire, you're so naïve." He smirked at her. "You're a suspect now, and the camera is mysteriously turned off. By the time you can find someone to lodge whatever complaint you think you deserve to, your paperwork will be long shuffled away, and no one will remember anything about this. Someone will check the camera and discover that no one knows how long it's had a short in the circuitry, because no one has subpoenaed the records in months."

There had to be some other thing she could say, some other way to get him to reconsider. "If you hurt me, Justin is going to kill you."

"He can try." Avery paced around the table and grabbed her yet again. Instead of hauling her to her feet as she expected, he jerked her up to smash her head into the table.

Claire squealed in surprise, then groaned in pain. He repeated the motion three times, then let her go to slump to the floor, the cuffs cutting into her wrists. She moaned and pressed her arms around her aching skull. "Please stop."

He crouched down and pressed a finger under her chin to force her to look at him. As soon as she met his gaze, he let go and slapped her hard enough to sting. "Tell me what he is to you. Why did he let you stay at his home?"

The question seemed too innocuous and he should already know the answer. Then again, Justin had to concentrate to see whatever marked her as a Knight, and he'd been surprised by it. Avery wouldn't think to check, and it might not change how he treated her anyway. "Because he's a nice guy."

"This is a simple question, Claire, and it's only going to get worse from here."

Her head hurt, and she wanted to make it stop. If he only promised to stop hitting her, she'd tell him anything and everything. But the casual way he banged her head and his sinister calm meant she wouldn't believe him even if he did promise that. "No."

"So be it."

CHAPTER 12

JUSTIN

"You should go talk to Kurt." Marie looped her arm through Justin's for the short walk home from her parents' house. They'd left the girls there and would pick them up again on Sunday afternoon.

"We have a rare weekend alone together, and you want to send me off?"

She grinned. "No. But you need to talk to him. You have that crinkle in your forehead."

"I don't have a crinkle."

"You do. It's right there." She tapped his head.

He reached up and rubbed the spot. "You just want me to go so you can invite all your friends over to have a pillow fight in lingerie without me."

"Tempting." She let go when he opened the door for her and

slipped out of her garden clogs in the entry. "I was actually thinking I might read a book without anyone interrupting me for an hour. I might even be convinced to do it in bed, wearing that red thing you like."

Wiping his boots on the outside mat, he smirked at her. "Or I could ravish you now and go tomorrow."

She waved him off and gave him a pleasant view of her back. Tight jeans hugged her wide hips, and she waggled her butt for him. "If you go now, though, I'll have time to get a surprise ready, and then you can laze about all day tomorrow."

He sighed. Once she'd made up her mind, it would take more than "I don't wanna" to change it. "Fine, woman. Don't fall asleep without me." Shutting the door on her laughter, he huffed another sigh and jogged to his tree. On the other side, he strode through the Palace, greeting others on his way to Kurt's room.

When he raised his hand to knock on the door for room 462, it opened, and a tall, dark-skinned Knight walked out. "Hey, Djembe."

Djembe held up a hand, and Justin backed away so he could close the door. He leaned in and spoke softly. "He hasn't got much time left." His accent revealed his Ethiopian childhood and British schooling.

Justin flicked his eyes to the door. Something squeezed his chest. "What do you mean? He was fine yesterday."

Djembe shook his head. "He crafted an illusion. A good one, and long-lasting. It took too much out of him. I think he's ready too."

"I'm not ready."

"Don't think that matters so very much, my friend." Djembe patted his shoulder. "Best to say goodbye while you can." He gave Justin a strained smile, then walked away.

Staring at the door, Justin rubbed his eyes. He'd always known this day would come, but why did it have to be now, when he needed advice? While the Palace had hundreds of other Knights to talk to about it, he didn't want any of them. Justin wanted the man who had put a weathered, calloused hand on his bewildered eighteen-year-old shoulder and explained that he couldn't hold down his regular job anymore, and they'd figure something out for his young wife and the child they were about to have.

Sucking up his pride and going to Marie's father had been Kurt's idea. He'd come along, even, and helped explain. Without his goading and presence, Justin's family would be living on the street or in a dingy little apartment, squeaking by on whatever he and Marie could somehow scrape together each month. Instead, Jack and Tammy let them live at the farm and use their electricity and water.

He knocked on the door and walked inside. The smell hit him first. It reminded him of visiting his grandmother at her nursing home before she died. Death hung in the air. Rounding the corner, he found Kurt sitting in his usual chair, a blanket covering his legs and his head resting against the cushion. Today he seemed more shriveled, as if the chair siphoned him away bit by bit.

Beside him, a beautiful woman sat in a folding chair, holding his hand. She looked up at Justin with a dazzling, ruby-red smile. "Kurt, you have another visitor." Her voice filled the room with a soft, sweet melody.

It took him a moment to remember that she couldn't be real. "Sorry to interrupt."

"Oh, don't you worry about it. Kurt can barely talk anymore, though." She brushed his cheek with her hand.

Kurt stirred. His mouth moved and only a bare hint of a whisper came out.

"He says he wishes you didn't have to see him like this, but he got a little carried away with the illusion. You can take the hat back whenever you want." Her gesture dragged his attention to the hat on the nightstand.

"Dammit." Justin hung his head and scratched the back of his neck. "I got myself an apprentice."

Kurt wheezed. It might have been laughter.

"Of course you did, boy." The words came out in the woman's voice, but he recognized Kurt in them. His mind, still sharp, must have been controlling her. "It's a circle. A wheel. What goes around comes around. I bet he's as much of a mess as you were."

He opened his mouth to correct Kurt's pronouns, then shut it. What good would that do? The old man could be dead any day now, and he might not be able to wrap his head around a girl as a Knight. Even if he could, Kurt would have to think about it. They might not have that much time. "You could say that."

"It's not rocket science, boy. Find him a place to feel safe, whether it's with you or not. Listen to what he says. Teach him what you know. Help him fix his problems without doing it for him. Simple. You'll be fine."

Nodding, he sighed. He'd muddle through somehow. Or Claire would bump into someone else here and decide he'd be a better mentor. Imagining her working with another Knight bothered him. He'd already opened his home to her and accepted responsibility for her. When he went to visit her next, he hoped she'd at least let him explain. If she wanted him to go away at that point, he'd leave. Maybe he could steer her in Avery's direction.

CHAPTER 13

CLAIRE

Claire lay curled up on the hard, flat shelf in a holding cell, stiff from having cried herself to sleep. Clutching her locket, she begged her father to give her strength. She didn't dare move, for fear of someone deciding she needed to go back to Avery. Everything hurt from head to toe. He'd taken her shoes, leaving her in knee-high orange and pink swirl socks, which had fallen to puddle around her ankles. One eye had swollen shut, and a scab crusted her lip.

She lay there, her thoughts scattered and incoherent, knowing only that Marie and the girls had been nice to her, and she wouldn't let him hurt them. They didn't deserve to have some lunatic cop storming their house and using them against Justin. Besides, Justin would come and rescue her, she knew it. If she held out long enough, he would come for her.

Footsteps scuffed down the concrete hall, putting tension in her shoulders. A heavy key ring jangled and clanged on metal. Hinges creaked. "On your feet," Avery barked.

"I can't," she breathed. In truth, she thought she could. Hope flickered in her chest. If she pretended to be more injured than she really felt, he might leave her alone or do something different.

"Try."

The undisguised menace in his tone made her push herself up enough to roll over. Her feet dangled from the bench. Was that too much? Her head *did* throb with a deep ache. The clank of handcuffs he'd promised not to use if she cooperated made her struggle to sit up. One more pathetic push sent her crumpling to the cold, hard floor at his feet.

"Oh, Claire." He sighed. "I really did expect more from you. With such a troubled childhood, you ought to be able to withstand a beating better than this." He grabbed the back of her shirt and picked her up with an ease that reminded her of Justin and his strength. The world spun and she wound up slung over his shoulder, her arms dangling and head pounding. Every step he took sent a jolt of agony into her belly that echoed in her skull.

She wanted to ask where he intended to take her but stuffed the question down in the hope he'd think she'd fallen unconscious. No one who passed them stopped him or asked any questions as he carried her down a flight of stairs and into a closet. When he shut the door, he dropped her onto the floor. Confused, she stayed limp in the dark, little room that smelled of bleach and ammonia, watching him through a curtain of hair.

He stayed there for two heartbeats, his eyes unfocused, then turned around and opened the door again. Everything was different. Instead of the hallway, she saw a star-filled night sky. Cool air blew into the cramped room. He grabbed her by the hair and yanked.

She squealed and grabbed his arm.

"Not as unconscious as you seem," Avery sneered. "Get up."

With the sharp pain in her scalp on top of everything else, she clambered to her feet and stumbled along behind him. "Is this the Palace?"

He stopped so abruptly that she walked into him and jerked her head forward. She whimpered and tried to look away from his suspicious glare. "What do you know about the Palace?"

That had been a stupid question to ask. Claire gulped and forced herself to breathe. "N-nothing. Justin mentioned it once, that's all."

"Why?"

She froze. "Uh."

He swept her legs out from underneath her and let go of her hair. She landed hard on her bottom and bit her tongue. As she groaned, he grabbed the front of her shirt and lifted his hand to strike her.

"Stop." The new voice sounded breathy and had a strange echo that made it seem to come from everywhere at once.

Avery shoved her to the ground instead of slapping her. Her hands hit the dark stone floor first, scraping already raw flesh and making her bleed. If he tried that again, she'd be ready to hit him back.

"What is this?" The new voice still had no source.

"Justin's taken her in." Avery shrugged. "I thought she might be useful in luring him to us or helping us find him."

"She's damaged."

"She's resisted helping me so far. I chose to employ enhanced interrogation techniques."

"And did that work?" The voice sounded familiar somehow, yet also distant and detached.

Avery glanced at her, his mouth drawing into a disappointed frown. "Not yet."

The air stirred with a warm, gentle breeze. "I...know you. Why do I know you?"

Claire looked for the source of the voice that resonated with her and saw no one. Wisping around her, the breeze pushed her chin up until she faced the sky. One pinprick of white light above widened until a pale beam enveloped her. A misty hand reached out and brushed her cheek.

"I know you." His face pushed into the light, as translucent as his hand.

She gasped. "Daddy?"

"Am I?" He frowned.

The force holding her head up faded away, and Claire stared at the fuzzy face of Mark Terdan, not knowing what to say or do. From Avery's treatment, she thought this place would hold something terrifying, something vengeful, hateful, and angry.

"It's Claire, Daddy."

"Claire." His form lost focus. "You're hurt." He took her hand and ice flooded into it. Cold sped up her arm, across her shoulder, and through her body. It shocked her pain away, then it receded, leaving her feeling whole again. "She will not be harmed again."

"Of course not," Avery said through clenched jaws. "She does know where to find Justin, though."

"Claire, we need to know where Justin is."

She wanted to believe him, and to believe in him. "Why? Aren't you both Knights? Can't you just go to the Palace thing and find him there?"

Mark turned to Avery. "What did you tell her?"

Avery crossed his arms and scowled. "Nothing. She spent the night with Justin. He must have told her things or let her overhear things."

"Spent the night?" Mark furrowed his brow as he turned to regard her again.

"I slept on his couch," she said with a roll of her eyes. "He's really happily married. They have little kids and everything."

Mark put his hands on her shoulders and met her eyes with a hard stare. "He's dangerous. Whatever he told you about the Knights, it's all a lie. They want to believe they're doing good, but the truth is, they're corrupting the land in a futile attempt to tame Phasms for their own purposes. Even Justin. Will you help us stop them?"

She gazed into her father's eyes and believed every word he said. Yet Justin had been nice to her, and she'd already been a pain to him. Even if he worked for the wrong team, he still had a great family. Avery couldn't be trusted to treat Marie and the girls with the kind of care they deserved. He'd already shown how he preferred to handle his problems.

"Something's not right with her." Avery crouched down and poked her arm. "The more I look at her, the more I think she's a budding Knight. But girls can't be Knights."

Mark smiled at her. "That's wonderful. My baby girl is going to be a Knight. No one needs to bother Justin, then. All you have to do is take something into the Palace and leave it in the main work room. You can do that, can't you?"

She blinked at him, confused. "Why?"

"To stop the Knights, of course."

Thinking back, she couldn't remember Justin saying anything about what the Knights actually did. She only knew it involved Phasms, and he seemed to know plenty about them. "To stop them from doing what? Are you going to hurt them?"

"No, of course not." Mark beamed at her. "It's good that you're concerned about them and their well-being. John, take her home and give her the item."

"As you wish," Avery said with a bow. "Come on, Claire, let's get you home." He set a heavy hand on her shoulder.

"But..." She threw her arms around her father's misty neck and hugged him. "I want to stay here with you, Daddy."

"I'm sorry, Claire." Mark pried her hands loose and nudged her away with a sad smile. "You can't. After the Knights are stopped, you can come stay with me, but not until then. For now, you have to wait for your power to grow until you can reach the Palace."

Her eyes burned with tears as Avery tightened his grip and dragged her away. "You left me all alone, Daddy. In the dark, with nothing but a stupid locket!"

She swore she saw her father's face furrow with confusion as Avery shut the door. "Wait," she begged.

Avery held her at bay with ease for two seconds, then he opened the door again to reveal the brightly lit police station hallway. He walked out without a backward glance.

Hugging herself, she crumpled to the floor. If this room could take her to her father, she had no reason to leave. All this time, he'd been in that strange, dark place. Had the Knights trapped him there? Justin had said he'd met Mark a few times. Did he mean he'd thrown her father into a dark pit for some reason?

"Claire." Avery crouched beside her and murmured close to her ear. "Get up and get moving, or we'll see how far I can push his orders not to harm you."

She sniffled. So many things confused her right now, but not this. If he said he'd hurt her, he meant he'd hurt her. She wiped her face and followed him out.

CHAPTER 14

JUSTIN

Leaning against the wall outside Kurt's room in the Palace, Justin stared at the flowered hat in his hands. Kurt's last breath had rattled out while Justin held his hand, then the illusion had unraveled. Now Kurt would be a Phasm someplace, probably in Portland. One duty taken away, another one added.

He'd do better with Kurt than he had with Mark. Two years ago, he'd lost track of Mark's Phasm and had no idea what had happened to it. Kurt hadn't been worried. Phasms don't get corrupted that often, he'd said. Justin remembered Kurt taking him to a stone cathedral in the city, one that had stood for a hundred years.

They walked into the church with Justin gawking like an idiot. His mother used to take him to church. She'd said she felt safe there but Justin never felt anything other than trapped inside that tiny, cramped hovel. This place, though, had a forty foot ceiling, stained glass windows, and warm honey-hued wood pews. Heavenly voices filled the air with a solemn hymn.

Once he crossed the threshold, he felt...something. This place had peace, a commodity in short supply in his life. The cathedral wanted him to be calm, content, and warm. That feeling reminded him of his mother too. As much as she'd been his safe haven, though, it had always been an illusion. His father had made certain of that.

"Men built this place with their hands," Kurt said, his voice hushed. "Phasms built this place too. I know you're really young to be thinking about your own death, but you need to know this stuff." He nodded to a pew near the back and set his aging bones on the seat.

Despite not wanting to linger, Justin dropped down beside him. Uncomfortable and trying to push away memories, he shut his eyes and rubbed them.

"When we die—Knights, I mean—we don't fully shuffle off like regular people. Every one of us creates a Phasm. It's an echo, a memory. An imitation made of mist. A ghost. Most of the time, a Phasm drifts around between places that were important in its life: home, school, work, maybe the graves of people it loved, that kind of thing. It never really catches on anything and eventually finds a place it can rest." Kurt held out his hands to show he meant the church.

"Houses of worship attract them, for some reason. They wind up in a place like this, and they settle. The longer they stay settled, the less recognizable they are. Eventually, they fade away until they're part of it and no longer separate. That's where this feeling comes from. Knights want to protect people. We keep wanting that even when we're dead.

"There's another thing that can happen to Phasms. When they're drifting, they can catch on something. Maybe it's a violent death, or a car crash, or a guy beating his wife."

Justin flinched, the wounds of his past still too raw to ignore.

Kurt either didn't notice or chose to ignore it. He already knew the worst parts. "They get fixated on that thing, and it keeps them from latching on to something harmless and fading. Instead, they get what we call 'corrupted.' They keep enough wits to come up with wild theories about how Knights are evil or destroying the world and eventually spawn their own domains, like the Palace, only specific to them. They see old friends as enemies and people they loved become distant tools."

"Sounds like we can be real dicks after death."

"Yeah. That's why living Knights hunt them down and forcibly dissipate them. I've handled several in my time. The last one was about two years ago. That's really the whole reason you have a sword, boy. That and the ne- and ur-phasms. The urs are little puffs of a Phasm's will, ones that find harmless looking animals and take them over. I don't know if cats and dogs have souls, but if they do, it gets booted out when an ur-phasm takes over. You can kill them without worrying about animal cruelty. And you'll be able to tell, because you'll understand them when they talk. The ne-phasms are even nastier, because they've tasted human essence and want more."

Up to now, the job hadn't sounded so bad, even with Tariel sassing him at every turn. This, though, confused him. "Why are there even Knights in the first place? It sounds like our whole purpose is to protect people from ourselves."

"I don't know, boy. Maybe someone at the beginning knew, but they didn't write it down or tell anyone." Kurt shrugged and looked around. The choir had stopped, and the cathedral filled with the sounds of their feet as the boys trooped away from the altar and through an ornate wooden door in the front of the building. "You hungry? I could go for some barbecue right about now."

Justin smirked. The old man had let his nose and belly lead him until he tripped and broke a hip. Then he'd withered away, unable to get up and about anymore. This stupid hat; Justin never should have stolen it. Without the hat, Kurt could've lived another few years. Then he remembered the smile on Kurt's face when he saw it and the love he'd put into crafting that illusion. In Kurt's place, he suspected he'd have done the same for Marie.

"Ah. I'm too late."

He looked up to see one of Kurt's friends approaching. The Jamaican elder Knight spent little time here, and Justin knew him only in passing. "Yeah. Sorry."

Rondy sighed and echoed Justin's pose against the opposite wall. "It's always hard to lose your mentor." He gripped Justin's shoulder and squeezed it. "If you ever need anything, just ask."

"Thanks." He mustered a somber smile and headed to the stairs. Rondy needed time to mourn too, and Justin had a family and an apprentice to take care of.

CHAPTER 15

CLAIRE

Claire lay on the soft pink floral sheets of her bed, clutching her stuffed white unicorn to her chest. It smelled of lavender and strawberry, a combination of Mom's soap and Claire's shampoo. Nothing else ever had that peculiar scent combination. She glanced at her corkboard closet door and noticed Brittney's latest letter pinned up alongside pictures from summer camp, a calendar flipped to September, and her own work from art class.

Mom had, yet again, turned down her request for an email address so she could send messages to Brittney. The other girl lived in Salem, much too far away to go see. Claire's half-finished return letter sat on her white desk with a sparkly purple pen lying across it. Now seemed like a good time to tell Brittney about the thing that had happened at school today.

She crossed the room, her toes sinking into the plush white carpet, and sat at her desk. The second her pen touched the paper, Tyler burst in, holding his blue plush airplane as high as his small arm could reach, providing engine noises with his mouth, and careening through her room. His interruption startled her, and she accidentally drew a long line across the page.

"Tyler," she groaned. "Get out of my room!"

He stuck his tongue out at her and ducked under her hand as she reached out to grab the airplane.

"Mom!" Claire jumped up and chased him out. "Make Tyler stay out of my room!"

"Can't catch me," he taunted between giggles.

"Oh yes I can!" Claire ran after him, tossing the unicorn aside. She chased him down the stairs and through the family room where her parents sat on the couch, curled up together and watching TV.

"Hey," Dad barked, "no running in the house! Take it outside."

Tyler skidded to a stop at the back door and yanked it open. Claire watched him run outside and stopped to stare at her parents. Both wore sweats and socks, usual attire for a lazy fall Saturday. Mom had her wavy black hair up in a ponytail. Dad hadn't bothered to comb his dark brown hair or to shave. The sight of them made her eyes burn.

No, that stinging was caused by the smoke billowing in through the open door. She coughed, and a wave of blistering heat rolled over her.

Her eyes snapped open, and she sucked in a lungful of pine-scented air. She'd fallen asleep in the back seat of Avery's car. The view out the window confused her. He shouldn't have needed to take the freeway to get her from the police station to her group home. "Where are we?"

She saw Avery look at her through the rearview mirror. "I'm taking you home."

"Are you taking the scenic route?"

"No."

She rubbed her eyes, thinking maybe the nightmare had scrambled her brains. "I don't understand."

"What's not to understand? I'm taking you home."

"Are you lost?"

"No." He snorted. "I drive this every day. Traffic is always crappy like this."

"Why do you drive to my foster home every day?"

He snorted again. "I'm taking you to *my* home, Claire, not yours."

"Oh." She leaned against the window, watching the scenery ooze past. Her father had only said "home" without specifying whose. She'd spend tonight locked up in a house with him. The meeting with her father ran through her mind and she realized this could last a lot longer than one night. Avery would keep her at his place until she mysteriously found her way to the Palace.

She wanted to find Justin. First, she needed to apologize for freaking out when he'd killed that cat. Second, she needed to know where he stood on the subject of "corrupting the land," whatever that meant. He might not really understand the Knights' purpose and goals. The guy couldn't have been doing it for long, so he might not have gotten inducted into the super-secret level of the group where they obviously would explain all that.

Avery left the freeway and drove into a dumpy apartment complex near the exit. For some reason, she'd expected him to have a big, fancy house with a manicured yard, in an upscale neighborhood. Brian seemed as though he'd live in a place like that. Avery parked in an underground garage and hauled her to the bare concrete stairs. They climbed up three flights, then he tossed her inside number twenty-seven.

Every surface was beige, white, or tan. He had a cheap plastic table and chairs, no dishwasher, and a ratty old couch opposite a big, boxy TV on stacked milk crates. Nothing was out of place, no mess had been left to fester. He kept his apartment simple and unadorned with no pictures or posters on the walls or table.

"Brian lives here?"

"No." His nostrils flared and his grip on her arm tightened. "He lives with his mother and little brother."

"Oh." Not wanting to anger him more, she dropped her gaze to the floor. "Sorry."

He grumbled without words and shoved her aside. "You can sleep on the couch."

She stumbled into the wall and rubbed her arm, expecting to have a hand-shaped bruise later. "Can I have my backpack?"

Scowling, he rolled his eyes. "It's in the trunk. Stay here and don't do anything stupid." He stalked out and slammed the door.

Blinking in surprise that he hadn't handcuffed her to something, she stared at the door. She could go walk right out the front door. And be completely lost, because she had no idea where this apartment complex was. Even if she found a bus stop nearby, she had no money to pay the fare. Her bus pass sat in the bottom of the very backpack she now waited for him to bring up.

Maybe it wouldn't be so bad here. She'd stayed in group homes where the foster parents hated kids. So long as everyone stayed quiet and did their homework and went to bed on time, everything was fine. The one she'd just moved into seemed like that. Avery was probably that kind of guy too.

She still wanted to talk to Justin without Avery around. Maybe she could sneak out in the middle of the night or get away from him tomorrow sometime. Or, she mused as she sank down to sit on his unexpectedly comfortable couch, she could try asking. "Hey, Avery," she asked the empty room with a smirk, "is it okay if I go out and wander around until I happen to bump into Justin?" Yeah, that would go over well.

Avery returned with her backpack, his brow climbing when he saw her sitting there. Maybe he'd expected her to run off. He dropped her pack onto the couch and crossed his arms. "You're probably hungry. Pizza or Chinese?"

"Um, pizza, I guess." She pulled her backpack to her chest and hunched her shoulders. "I like mushrooms."

The corners of his mouth tugged down as he pulled out his phone. "Is pepperoni okay?"

"Sure." She listened to him order a pepperoni pizza with mushrooms and wondered if this man might be the good twin of the cop who had beaten the crap out of her. Confused by him, she pulled her locket out and rubbed it.

Avery hung up his phone and turned to leave the room. As he reached the back hall, he glanced at her with his mouth open to say something and froze. "What's that?"

The question startled her. She tucked the locket under her shirt again. "Nothing."

He crossed the room in two steps and grabbed her arm, forcing her to her feet. "Show it to me," he snarled.

Shocked by the sudden return of the scary creep from that interrogation room, she cringed away from him. "Leave me alone," she whimpered.

Raising his hand, he bared his teeth and clearly had to restrain himself from hitting her. He growled in the back of his throat and snagged a fistful of her shirt, pulling it down hard enough to rip the shoulder seam.

This time, he hadn't handcuffed her to keep her from fighting back. She swung at his face but he dodged the blow with ease. At the same time, though, she kneed him in the groin; he clearly hadn't expected *that*. His eyes bugged out, and she swung again, hitting him in the gut. The second his grip loosened, she snatched up her backpack and fled the apartment.

Her father had chosen a crappy champion. Slinging her pack on her back, she ran up the hall, took the stairs down, and burst out through the front door. When she reached the parking lot, she found his car trundling through the parking lot, waiting for her. There had to be another way to go. Checking all around for one, she caught sight of Avery on his balcony, wheezing and climbing over the railing to jump down.

The car gunned its engine and squealed its tires. Claire ran. She ducked between parked cars and covered her head when she heard metal and glass crunch and smash behind her. Risking a glance over her shoulder, she saw Avery's car had plowed into the parked cars and now was backing up, looking none the worse for the impact.

With a gulp, she darted away from the complex as fast as she could. Panic gave her speed. Hurtling around a corner, she wished Justin would show up to rescue her already. He'd failed at that so far. A guy like that ought to magically show up whenever she wound up in danger. Instead, she kept having to rescue herself and so far, she'd done an absolutely bang-up job of it. He needed to show up and do it right.

The car screamed around the corner and roared after her as she dashed up the sidewalk. Other cars drove past and she prayed for Avery's sprite to let her go rather than risk being seen by normal people. Brakes squealed behind her and she heard the explosive impact of two cars. Screaming metal made her glance over her shoulder. The lunatic car now pushed a twisted wreck at her like a battering ram. Other cars on the road swerved and braked to avoid it.

She squeaked in panic and ran across the street under an overpass, trusting the drivers to brake when they saw the mad car. Across the street, she heard more smashing, squealing, and shrieking. This time, she focused on breathing, on running, on getting away from that thing. On the other side of the overpass, she scrambled up the embankment and found a freeway onramp.

The demented car would have no trouble catching her up here. She ran across the bridge and saw a truck coming in the one remaining clear lane underneath. Avery's car lurched up the onramp, metal scraping the road and throwing orange sparks. No one on a freeway would stop to help her. In seconds, the car would reach her. She noticed this overpass didn't have the usual fencing along the side.

Desperate to escape, she took a deep breath and leaped over the side, hoping this would work half as well as it did in the movies.

CHAPTER 16

JUSTIN

"This is a stupid idea."

"That's why it's going to work."

"That's even more stupid." Tariel trotted along the street, keeping up with traffic in downtown Portland.

"No one expects the dumb move. It's like the Spanish Inquisition." Justin almost smiled. He'd spent half an hour figuring out how to word a note about what had happened to the hat and who it had belonged to. Now he had both it and the hat clutched in one hand as they headed for the Oregon Historical Society. He'd like to keep it, as a memento of Kurt, but they'd take better care of it.

Tariel rolled her eyes, showing the whites. "One of these days, you're going to get us both killed."

"Probably. Until then, just remember that *you* chose *me*."

"To my eternal dismay." The horse whuffed out a long-suffering sigh. "I wonder what'll chose Claire."

"We should go see her after this. We're already missing dinner, so we might as well go all in and see if I can get screamed at by as many women as possible."

"Go big or go home." Tariel chuckled.

"Damn straight." He sighed. "What do you think about that, anyway? Claire being a Knight, I mean."

Her ears flicked. "It's... I think you should bring another Knight to have a look at her. That would also give her another ally in the Palace when she does cross over. You don't spend a huge amount of time there, after all. She probably will."

Looking down at the hat, he nodded. As much as he wanted to be her mentor, he had to admit she'd be in a much better position if she collected a number of allies. "That's a good idea. We'll swing over to her foster home after this and see if she'll listen. If not, we'll leave and I'll go grab someone."

They turned up Park Avenue, following traffic flow on the south-bound side. Tariel turned onto the green strip behind Teddy Roosevelt and crossed the north-bound lane, then let him off at the front door. He grabbed the handle, yanked it open, and strode inside. The man working behind the front desk happened to be the gentleman who'd been there the other day, and now he had a line of people waiting to pay to get in.

"Excuse me." Justin walked past the line to set the hat and note on the counter.

The man stared at him, blinking rapidly. "Uh?"

"I apologize for taking this and hope it wasn't damaged beyond repair. The note details its exploits, which I suspect will enrich the museum more than the temporary loss of the hat detracted from it." With that, he gave the man a polite smile and left. Everyone stared at him, watching as he walked out the front door, climbed onto Tariel's back, and rode up the street.

A few blocks away, with no sirens to be heard, he grinned. "See? It worked."

"Great," Tariel groused. "One dumb plan worked, so now you'll be an insufferable idiot forever."

Justin laughed. "I love you too."

CHAPTER 17

CLAIRE

The group home had never looked more inviting than it did when Claire reached it that evening. Limping, on the run from a small pack of crazed dogs, and bruised all over, she stumbled inside the front door and slammed it shut, then leaned against it. Now that she'd made it here, she needed to figure out what to do. As the truck carried her far away from both Avery and his sprite, she'd been trying to come up with someplace safer to go.

No matter how much she trusted her father, nothing would make her accept Avery as her keeper. Whenever she got the magic pass into the Palace, she'd go find Avery and make him give her the item. She'd be a Knight then, and he wouldn't be able to beat her up again. The more she thought about it, though, the more she wondered why Avery didn't take the thing to the Palace himself. As a Knight, he should be able to do that.

From the dining room, she heard a chair scrape on the floor and the sound motivated her to move again. She hurried to her room, hoping to avoid questions. Leaving Drew behind would suck for both of them, but at least he'd be safe here until all this crazy stuff stopped.

"Claire!" The foster father's voice boomed through the house, making her flinch.

Like everyone else staying here, she kept her wheeled suitcase packed at all times with as little as possible sitting out. She only needed to grab the wad of dirty clothes in her laundry bag, her coat, and her threadbare white unicorn. With everything stuffed into the suitcase, she zipped it up and wheeled it out of the bedroom. The foster father filled the hallway, standing between her and escape.

"Don't even try to stop me. I've got somewhere else to go now." She had no idea where that somewhere else might be, only that it would be better and safer than this one.

"We got a call you got arrested." His onion, garlic, and potato breath assaulted her.

"I'm free now, and I'm outta here. Keep collecting the checks for all I care." She stepped up and got into his face, daring him to stop her.

"You're not old enough to go out on your own." He planted his large fists on his wide hips. "If you're running away, I'm locking you in."

She glared at him. "You're gonna need handcuffs and duct tape to keep me here, you fat bastard."

He smacked her across the face hard enough that she let go of her suitcase, then he grabbed her around the neck. "Wrong answer. Let's go, Princess." He dragged her out of the room and down the hall. "Why is there always a troublemaker? Every single time we get a batch of new kids, there's always one that can't be bothered to just go to school, stay out of trouble, and follow the rules. I don't think we have really awful rules here, either. Some places, they lock up the food, decide when you can use the bathroom, that kind of thing. All we ask is you be home by dark, sit down to meals with everyone else, and let us know ahead of time if you won't. That's really not so bad, all things being equal."

As he hauled her along, Claire struggled against his beefy arm, gasping for breath and digging her heels into the rug. After everything that had happened over the past few days, this turn of events seemed so unbelievable that she had no idea what to do about it. He flung the closet door open and squatted down to grabbed the handle of a trapdoor and heave it up.

"Watch out, Princess, the first step is a doozy." He shoved her at the dark hole in the floor. She grabbed the edges, kicked at him, and squirmed. He growled and wrestled with her until he managed to loop his arm around her neck and choked her. Her vision faded and she went limp. The world spun as he tossed her in. Dazed, she landed in a heap on a sheet of plastic and groaned.

Her neck ached and her cheek hurt. Rage boiled out of her in a wordless scream at the world. The moment she got her wits back, she surged to her feet in the four-foot high crawlspace and thumped her shoulder into the trap door. It didn't budge. She tried again and again, accomplishing nothing except hurting her shoulder. "I didn't get through all of that to be stopped by you!"

Something thumped on the floor above and the foster father's muffled voice shouted, "Shut up, kid!"

"Go to Hell, you sonofabitch." Ignoring another thump on the floor, she took a tour of her new prison. She had no hope of getting her head through the tiny vents to the outside, let alone her shoulders. At least that meant Avery couldn't use them to get in, either. Of course, if he came to the house and they told him where to find her, she couldn't escape.

Seeing no way out, she screamed again and dropped down under the trapdoor to cry. Someone thumped on the floor again. The second that trapdoor opened for any reason, she'd surge up to kick, bite, and claw her way out. Justin hadn't come before and he wouldn't come now. He wasn't Superman, and she wasn't Lois Lane.

She pulled her locket out to rub her thumbs over it and press it to her cheek. Daddy would find a way to get her out of this, even if it meant sending Avery. He'd open the door and help her out, then she'd kick him in the shins and run away again. This time, she'd take all her stuff and go someplace unexpected to hide.

She curled up in a ball and waited in the near-dark, unable to guess how much time passed before chairs scraping and thumping overhead turned into the front door opening and shutting, then the younger kids playing tag outside.

"Psst, Claire."

She looked up, confused by the whisper. "What?"

"Ssh! It's Drew. Outside."

Her heart thumped so hard she thought she might throw up. She scrabbled to the wall and checked vent after vent until she found him peering through the screen. That stupid mesh needed to go so she could touch him. She punched through it and reached for him.

He smiled at her and squeezed her hand. "There's a weird guy with a horse here. Says he's looking for you but isn't talking to the fosters."

Claire's heart leaped into her throat. He came! Somehow, he figured out to come here. "He's my friend. Tell him where I am. Please?"

"What's he want?"

"To rescue me. Drew, you gotta tell him where I am. I gotta get out of here. There's someone who wants to hurt me, and this guy wants to help. I think he might adopt me, or maybe his parents will."

Drew gulped. "Okay, but I'm coming with you."

"No, you can't. You have to stay here and be safe. Please, Drew. I won't be able to think straight if you're not safe."

"Tell me how to find you." His words came out strangled and tortured. "I can't let you go again, not like last time."

Tears stung her eyes at the thought of losing him forever. "Stay here and I'll find you when I can. I promise I'll come back for you."

Drew squeezed her hand again. "Promise on their graves."

"I promise on the graves of my parents and brother that I'll come back for you."

He looked away and nodded, wiping his face with his sleeve. "Okay. I'll tell him." He squeezed her hand again, then let go and ran off. A few seconds later, she heard his voice, muffled by distance, along with another male voice. She tucked the locket under her shirt again and stood up, too nervous, excited, confused, and angry to sit still anymore. Hunched over, she paced, waiting for him to rescue her. She heard rapping on the front door and rushed to that end of the house. The door opened. Everything took forever.

"Hi there. I'm here for Claire."

"I don't know you," the foster father said, "and don't let costumed freaks inside my house. Get off the porch and get out of here or I'll call the police."

Justin snorted. "Let me rephrase. I know she's in the basement, and you can either get her and bring her to the door, or I'll use my horse and sword to put a hole in your wall and floor to get her out myself. Your choice."

"Mabel," the foster father's voice shouted, "ca—*glrk*!" Claire heard shuffling and grunting, and had no idea what to make of all the noise. Something big and heavy hit the floor and boots clomped into the kitchen.

"Ma'am, I didn't come here to destroy your home or seriously injure anyone, but I will if you force me to. Put the phone down and show me the basement access."

Other feet scuffed on the floor. "It's down there," Drew said with an unhappy sigh. "This is her suitcase."

"Thanks." She followed the sound of Justin's boots to the trap door. It got heaved aside and light streamed in as Justin smiled down at her. "Claire, I came to apologize."

She burst into tears, so happy to see him she couldn't speak.

"Are you hurt?" He reached for her, and when she wrapped her arms around his neck, he lifted her out.

"You came," she bawled into his shoulder, still holding on and not caring about the hard metal of his pauldrons.

"Of course I came. Can you walk?"

"I'm sorry. I shouldn't have done that, but I did, and you still came anyway, and I'm sorry."

"Claire." He pushed her away from him and put a finger under her chin to make her meet his eyes. "It's okay. It was my fault too. We'll talk about it later. Right now, we need to leave. Mabel's probably calling the cops right now because a sword-wielding freak punched her husband in the face and he's still out cold."

"Actually," Mabel's voice said from behind him, "considering how much effort you put into coming for Claire, and how happy she is to see you, I'm inclined to let you have a head start. So long as I shouldn't be worried about an inappropriate relationship, given your apparent age and all."

Justin grinned. "I'm happily married to someone else, ma'am. We're hoping to take her in as a big sister for our little girls."

Claire beamed, delighted to hear she had a home waiting for her. "Really?" Over Justin's shoulder, she saw Drew break into a relieved smile too. Meeting his eyes, she mouthed the words "Vancouver" and "Brady farm."

"Yes, really. We'll talk about that later too."

"Then Godspeed," Mabel said with a smile, "and good luck." She offered Claire a tissue. "I'll handle my husband, you get going. And do up the paperwork properly as soon as you get a chance."

"Yes, ma'am. Thank you." He pulled Claire up to her feet, took her hand, and led her out. Along the way, Claire grabbed her suitcase from Drew and rolled it along behind her. She had to pick it up to get around the foster father, still lying in the hall, then she was free of this place forever. Drew stood in the doorway and blew her a kiss. She caught it and tried not to be upset about leaving him behind.

CHAPTER 18

JUSTIN

Tariel trotted along with traffic on the city streets, taking them home. Justin had one arm wrapped around Claire, holding her tight. She seemed so upset, but being locked in the basement shouldn't have been so horrific. According to the boy, she'd only been down there for half an hour. Worse, she had a limp, and her clothes were ripped up.

"Claire, you look like hell. What happened?"

She looked up at him with needy red eyes and puffy cheeks, hints of purple coloring one side of her face. "I met my dad."

That must have been confusing for her, and distressing. It didn't explain the bruises, but he'd let her get to that in her own time. "Oh. Ah. How's his Phasm doing?"

Her eyes watered and she sniffled. "It was like touching something without touching it." She paused and sniffled more. He waited. "He said the Knights need to be stopped. But I don't understand why he needs me to do it when he has Avery."

His blood ran cold. A curse slipped out of his mouth, and he knew without a doubt that whatever had happened to Claire over the past two days had all been his own stupid fault. He should have kept better track of Mark's Phasm. He should have kept in touch with Avery. He should have checked up on her last night.

Too late for any of that. Now he had to deal with it all. He also had to explain what he'd seen to Claire, and it would break her heart. For that, they needed to stop and settle in someplace where Avery and none of Mark's pets could find them. "Tariel, take us across the river so we're out of any Oregon police jurisdiction, and go north. Don't go near the farm."

The horse sped up, and he covered Claire with his cloak when they joined the freeway. They went up Interstate 5 past Vancouver, taking the Kelso exit and heading east, away from the town. At the end of a road, Tariel jumped over a hedge line and landed on damp, spongy earth. They traveled through thick trees, leaves dripping in a light ran. Justin wiped his face, soaking wet from the neck up.

Half an hour later, Tariel stopped and Justin flicked the cloak aside to let Claire see where they were. The horse stood in front of a dark cleft in a rocky hillside, one with a floor sloping up and enough space to hold a bear. Runnels of water ran down around the hole without dribbling inside it. Tariel would be stuck in the rain, but they wouldn't.

He climbed down and put a hand out to prevent Claire from following. It almost surprised him to see her obediently stay on Tariel's back. To be on the safe side, he pulled out his sword. The metallic ting as it scraped against the scabbard bounced off the cave walls, echoing deeper in.

Peering into the gloom, he braced for a possible onrush of angry animals or ur-phasms. "Anybody in there?" His voice sent a second echo chasing the first.

When he heard a chorus of screeches, he stood away from the hole and waited. Bats streaked out, disturbed by his intrusion. One in the middle separated from the flock and dove at Claire. Of course there had to be an ur-phasm in the group. Tariel snapped at it, Claire covered her head and Justin ducked under the swarm. The ur-phasm flapped around, shrieking in unintelligible anger. It took him two swings before he caught the thing in midair and sliced it in half.

Tariel had the presence of mind to move her head so it blocked Claire's view of the bleeding corpse. "How refreshing. It's been a while since ur-phasms blindly attacked us."

Justin snorted and used his cloak to clean his blade.

"What the—?" Claire looked up and her still-red eyes went wide as she watched the blood rolling down his cloak with the water. She gulped. "Um, your cloak?"

He shrugged. "It's magic."

"Really?" She climbed down from Tariel's back and grabbed a corner of his cloak to rub the fabric between her fingers. "It's not just, like, water-repellent flannel?"

"Yes, it's really magic." He grinned. "Your dad had one a lot like it. The sword and armor too. You'll be able to make your own when you get to the Palace, though we'll hold off on that until you've had a little time to adjust to the place."

Claire's eyes slid to the sword. "Can I...?"

Justin's brow raised, then he handed the hilt of the blade to her.

"Some Knights make them really fancy. I'm more of a 'walk in the front door' kind of guy."

"She thinks you mean that figuratively." Tariel's eyes danced with merriment.

He stuck his tongue out at the horse and thanked everything in existence that no one else would ever understand her. "You'll be able to make yours look however you want. Your father, if I recall correctly, preferred something in between. It had a fancy silver guard with a thick blade, and he etched a design along the center of the blade. No gemstones or anything like that."

She gripped the leather-wrapped T-shaped hilt and ran her fingertips along the plain steel blade. "What happened to it?"

"It dissipated when he died. If you want a copy of it, the Palace has a memory for that sort of thing. There are guys walking around with copies of swords from a thousand years ago."

Her eyes unfocused, and her voice came out breathy and distant. "I always thought his sword was fake. A prop."

"He wanted to shield you from the unpleasant things he sometimes had to do." It seemed unwise to leave a large, sharp weapon in the untrained hands of a distracted teenager for long, so he gripped the blade with his gauntlet and tugged it away from her.

Her attention snapped back to him and she narrowed her eyes. "Like what?"

Frowning, he sheathed the sword and stalked into the cave. Five paces in, he found rocks at the right height for sitting and used one. Claire followed him in, then remained standing with her fists on her hips. This time, she wouldn't be distracted from the subject. He sighed and told her the generic things Kurt had told him about Phasms.

She softened and sat opposite him as she spoke. "So my dad will fade away at some point and make someplace better?"

Unable to look at her while he said this, he let his thumbs attract his attention. "No. I need to go back to the Palace to be sure, but I'm pretty confident the entity that looks like your father is a corrupted Phasm."

"But..." She gulped. "How can you know that without meeting him?"

"It's a common thing for a corrupted Phasm to think the Knights need to be stopped. A lot of them scheme and plot to destroy the Palace, or to kill Knights. It's very likely that he's managed to taint Avery."

"But he could—"

"No, Claire, he couldn't. He's corrupt, I promise. It's not your dad, it's an echo of him, one that's gotten confused and twisted. I'm going to have to hunt it down and destroy it. If I leave it, people will get hurt."

"He said..." She wiped her face. "You're really sure?"

"I'm sorry." He nodded and let his shoulders sag. "It's my fault you had to meet it. And I shouldn't have killed that ur-phasm cat in front of you the other day. That was dumb."

She covered her face, and her shoulders shook. For a heartbeat, he hesitated, then he shifted to her rock and put an arm around her shoulders. Leaning into him, she sobbed. He held on and let her weep for as long as she needed to. Her pain and grief, so easily expressed, made him wonder if the weight of Kurt's death had yet to settle on his own shoulders.

When her tears subsided and finally straightened away from him, he let her decide what she wanted from him. It turned out to be nothing for several minutes. When Marie had learned about her first pregnancy, she'd wanted quiet and distance. She'd needed time to deal with it herself before letting him back in. Then, he'd thought it a rejection. Now, he knew better.

"A few days after they all died, I went to my first group home." She stared at her feet, her voice thick. "The foster mom there told me all the rules, then she took me to a bunk bed in a big room and said I had to take the top, because it was the only one they had. All the kids under twelve slept in the same room, and the bunk below me belonged to an eleven-year-old boy.

"I dreamed that night that my dad came on his big horse and apologized for the misunderstanding and all the pain of those few days. He had an enemy who needed to believe we were all dead, and it worked, and now he could come get me and we'd all be together again, in a new house. Then I woke up in that place and I cried.

"I guess I was kind of loud. The boy below me climbed up and held on to me and told me his parents had been dead for three years already, and it would get better, and all kinds of other stuff. He turned twelve a few days later and moved into the older boys' room. Sometimes he'd sneak back into the kids' room and stay with me until I fell asleep."

He stayed quiet for several moments after she finished, considering it a gesture of trust that she'd tell him something so personal. It felt like a story that demanded reciprocation, but he wasn't ready to share his own with her. Maybe later. "You were lucky to find someone to connect with in the system."

Claire took a deep breath and nodded. She hugged herself, then dropped her arms, then stood and wound up staring out at Tariel. "How long will we stay here?"

"Until we have a plan." He finally pulled his chain gloves off. They hit the floor of the cave with a wet splat. Their magic had, of course, kept his hands dry. He had to think now, to decide what to do about Mark and Avery.

"Did you mean it when you said that you wanted to have me as a big sister for Missy and Lisa?"

The question took him off guard. "Yes," he blurted. Except he and Marie hadn't talked about it yet. "Maybe. I don't know." The filtered light showed him how she bit her lip, anxious and waiting for him to crush her dreams. Or maybe that was him projecting. "It feels weird to ask if you want Marie and I to adopt you when you're not even ten years younger than us." He scraped a hand through his hair. Marie wouldn't argue much, and if she did, he'd talk her into it. "Would you like us to adopt you, or would you rather talk to Marie's parents about it?"

"Really? I get to choose between either being adopted or being adopted?"

He chuckled. "I suppose that's one way to put it. Jack and Tammy would have an easier time with the paperwork, since they aren't wanted for any crimes or anything, but we'd be happy to have you, if that's what you want. I think Lisa and Missy both like you. It is a farmhouse, so there'd be chores, of course. And a new school, and switching to a different state and all that. Anyway, think about it. We'll have to have a big family meeting to see what everyone thinks, but you have a place with us one way or another, no matter what."

Claire's face lit up with a wide smile. "Wow. I just—wow. Yeah. Okay. I, um, I don't even know what to say?"

"How about..." He tapped his chin, pretending to think about it.

"'Let's make a plan, dumbass, so we can sort this out as soon as possible and then deal with it after'?"

She fell over laughing. "Yeah, that's probably a good idea," she gasped out between giggles.

"I agree." He watched her continue to giggle with an amused smirk. "First, I need to go to the Palace to double-check that Avery's no longer a Knight. If he's still a Knight, I can talk to him and figure out what's going on. He's probably not, though. Where did he take you to meet the Phasm?"

"The police station. He dragged me into some closet and then opened the door again and it was night someplace. That's where my—the Phasm was. He healed me there."

CHAPTER 19

CLAIRE

Justin froze in the act of standing up. "Wait. What? He *healed* you?"

The way he asked, filled with horror and outrage, batted Claire's joy aside and made her shrink away from him. "Yeah. Um, Avery tried to, uh, *convince* me to tell him your address or last name or something."

His face went hard and angry. "If anyone ever hits you again, and you can't take care of it yourself, you tell me about it."

She gulped. "Okay." Taking a deep breath, she told him how it all happened, from the moment she met Avery in the principal's office to the part where Justin opened the trapdoor at the group home. He simmered with rage through the whole story.

"That sonofa—" He clenched his jaws together and punched the rock wall with enough force to make Claire wince in sympathy though it didn't seem to have hurt him. "Avery is a dead man. Aside from that, he's got your blood, and that's a problem. A corrupted Phasm can bind you with it. A tainted Knight can track you with it."

Even without knowing what he meant by "bind," she felt shocks of panic spark to her fingers and toes. "What do we do?"

He crossed his arms and glowered at the wall. "First, we have to keep you moving. I can't take you home until one of them is dead." He paced deeper into the cave, then returned and kept going back and forth. "Neither can track you on their own. Avery has about twenty years more experience than me, so he'll be harder to handle. The Phasm is in a pocket of its own making, so it'll be harder to find and get at."

Facing Avery again sounded awful. Having to slay her own father would be worse. But, she reminded herself, it wasn't her father. Mark Terdan died six years ago in a house fire. This thing was only a ghostly echo of him. She rubbed her face. "What do you need me to do?"

"I should get help, but I can't leave you alone for that long. Dammit, I wish you'd hurry up and get to the Palace."

"Me too."

"Okay." He stopped beside her, vibrating with frantic energy. "Do you remember where Avery's apartment building was?"

"No. Sorry." She hung her head.

"Alright. Then we can either taunt Avery or you can pretend to cooperate."

She jerked her head up, surprised, pleased, and nervous. It sounded as though he wanted her to choose. Maybe if she understood all this stuff, she'd feel competent to make a decision. To steady herself, she drew her locket up out of her shirt and rubbed it. "Which one do you think is better?"

Justin opened his mouth, then he squinted at her hand. "What's that?"

"This? It's the locket my parents gave me." She held it up so he could see it.

Taking it in his fingertips, he frowned. "Did either the Phasm or Avery see it?"

She shifted, wishing she could forget Avery ripping her shirt and hoping she hadn't done anything wrong. "Why?"

"Tariel, come look at this. Can I borrow it for a moment? I'll give it right back."

White-hot panic roared over her body, and she yanked it away from him. "No!"

Blinking, he stared at her and raised both hands in surrender. "Ooookaaaay." The horse whickered from the cave mouth and Justin shrugged. "No idea. Claire, I don't want to take the locket, I just want to look at it. May we look at it, please?"

The queer panic receded and she blinked, not sure what just happened. "Um, sure." Shuffling forward, she held the pendant up for them to see with it still around her neck.

"What was that about?" Justin used one finger to hold it up for Tariel. The horse pushed her nose into the cave and whuffed at the locket.

"I...don't know. The idea of taking it off..." Claire swallowed, queasy for no reason. "I've never taken it off. Ever. Not to sleep or shower or anything. Please don't make me take it off."

"I won't. I promise." He listened to the horse whinny and whicker. "Why didn't we see that before?" The horse said something else, and he nodded. "That makes sense."

"I'm glad it makes sense to you," Claire grumbled.

He let go of the locket and it thumped back against her chest. "We think it was made in the Palace. If your father gave it to you, it should have dissipated when he died. Because it didn't, there's something more to it. Tariel thinks this might be what makes it appear you're going to be a Knight."

"Which means what?"

"I don't know." He frowned and went to pick up his gauntlets. "Best guess? Your father did something he wasn't supposed to be able to." Like his cloak, his gauntlets appeared to be dry as he pulled them on. "I can think of three reasons I'd be willing to try that: Marie, Lisa, and Missy. If any of them were in danger of dying, I'd do anything to save them. Including secretly crafting a locket and binding it to their soul." She watched him walk out of the cave and brush water off Tariel's saddle, then climb up to settle there.

"And that means...?" Not wanting to be left here, she followed and looked up at him, not sure she wanted to know the answer.

"If the locket comes off your neck, you die. Also, it's the reason you're going to be a Knight. We didn't notice it because you keep it under your shirt, and we didn't think to check for an object. As far as I know, that's never happened before. Whatever makes us Knights is supposed to be part of us, not something external." He held out a hand to help her up.

"He gave me this locket because I was going to die? But I've had it for as long as I can remember." She took his hand and climbed up to sit in front of him.

"If it kept that memory, the Phasm might know what happened. In that case, it'll realize it only needs the locket to get to the Palace. It'll do anything to get it, including kill you." He reached around her to pick up Tariel's reins and held Claire close.

Her father's arms had felt like this: warm, safe, secure. She grabbed a handful of Tariel's mane. "But if my dad did something impossible to save my life, wouldn't he still want to save my life?"

"If he made the locket himself, yes. Tariel, take us to Portland. We've got to figure out how to handle this before I can come up with a more specific destination."

The horse whinnied and trotted through the woods. Claire pulled her locket out again and wondered what had happened all those years go to make her father have to do so much to save her. Her head filled with horrific accidents and diseases, then the images grew more sinister.

"Do you think one of these Phasm things went after me to get to him?"

"I really have no idea what happened. I only met him a few months before he died, and we didn't spend much time together. He wasn't my mentor." He sighed. "I'm sorry I can't tell you stories about him, or about you."

She wanted to hug him and frowned because she couldn't right now. After going through so much crap in his own life, he shouldn't have to be the rock that everyone leaned on and no one propped up. She considered patting or squeezing the arm he held around her and rejected that idea. The last thing she wanted was to make him think she might be crushing on him. That would make for awkward conversations and situations.

Besides, she had Drew. Maybe he'd consider letting Drew in, the same way Jack had let Justin in. If they could find someplace for both of them to sleep. As much as she desperately wanted to be part of Justin's family, she felt a pang of guilt for the space and food, and everything else she'd take up in their lives without giving much back.

The rain had stopped, and they reached the road. Tariel clopped down it under an overcast sky. Claire watched the trees give way to houses, then businesses. Gray clouds trundled past, and she caught sight of a patch of blue sky.

As they headed for a freeway onramp, Justin sighed with a grumble. "We have no good options, so we're taking a lousy one."

Tariel sped up, leaving Claire wondering how the horse knew where to go. Half an hour later, she had a guess. Another five minutes after that, she knew her guess had been right and had no idea what to think. "What are we doing here?"

Justin pulled on the reins to get Tariel to turn into the parking lot at Grant High. "Where else would you like to look to find Avery's home address?"

"The Internet?"

"Would we also be able to pick up your stuff there?"

Claire opened her mouth, then shut it, unable to think of a snappy comeback. She did already have her backpack, but she wouldn't mind grabbing the bag she kept in her locker. Instead, she focused on the reasons this wouldn't work. "Two things. One, Avery is divorced and his kids live with his ex-wife. Two, it's Saturday. Everything is locked up. How're you going to get in?"

"Universal opening tool." He hopped off Tariel's back when she stopped and pulled his sword out. "It slices, it dices, it juliennes, all for the unbelievably low price of never being able to hold down a regular job. As for the first point, I'll bet his ex-wife knows where he lives, and she can probably tell us about him."

"Whoa, Choppy McChop-chop." Claire tried to follow him to the ground, but the horse perfectly foiled her efforts by hopping and sidestepping. "Hey! Look, Justin, I go to school here. You don't have to carve it up. Besides, you've already got cops on your trail. Do you really need to add another reason for them to come down on you? There's got to be another way."

He turned and fell into a pose she thought she'd seen on a movie poster. It made him seem heroic and incredible, and she had no idea how a girl like her had managed to get a guy like him to watch over her. "That may be. Do you have any thoughts on this other way?"

She blinked at him as the moment passed. He still didn't quite seem real. "Uh. Er?"

"That's what I thought. And you won't be going to school here anymore." He returned to swaggering toward the building, cloak swishing behind him, blade gleaming in the fleeting sunshine. With a slash of his sword, he cut around the lock in the front door. He pushed and the door swung open.

Dumbstruck by his bold, brash action, she gaped. Then she noticed which part of the school they'd arrived at and tapped on the horse's neck. "You know he's never been here before, right? I mean, sure, I've only been here a few times and all, but at least I know where stuff is. He just broke into the gym. The office is over there." She pointed for the horse's benefit. "Can I get down now, please?"

Tariel tossed her head and whickered, then dropped her hind quarters. Claire hopped off. In the doorway, she paused long enough to admire the strength of his sword. It had made a clean cut through a steel door without screeching or forcing him to wrench it. The blade probably couldn't be stopped. She gulped, imagining him using it on a person. They'd be sliced in half as easily as this door had been. Gross.

She found him in the hall. "Good thing you didn't call this plan 'brilliant.' Did you not go to high school? Or just forget what the parts look like?"

"I figured it's all connected, and your locker might be in one of the other parts. Besides—" he grinned "—it's kind of fun to cut doors like that, and I don't get to do it very often. Is there a different door I can cut now?"

"Seriously?"

Justin laughed. "Come on, show me the way."

"Aren't you worried about ur-phasms jumping us in here?"

"No. It's a school. Phasms can't infest schools or hospitals. I was under the impression they couldn't get into police stations, either, but that seems to not be true. Or, at least, it's not as true as I've been led to believe."

They reached the part of the building with her locker, and she struggled over the combination before pulling out her electric blue bag with spare clothes, granola bars, and a money pouch. "This is all I want from here."

"Aren't you going to take these?" He pointed to the textbooks still piled in her locker.

"Ew, no. Why? They aren't even mine. I was issued them. Like I want to steal my Chemistry book or something." She left the locker door hanging open to make things easier on whoever had to clean it out.

"I did alright in Chemistry. It's not *that* bad."

Claire rolled her eyes and led the way to the office. "Pretty sure whatever new school I wind up at will have their own books. Vancouver is across the state line and all." They reached the office without him making any further disparaging comments, and she had to wonder if being in a high school brought out his inner smartass.

Justin's eyes lit up at the sight of the locked office door and he sliced it open the same way as he had the gym door. This time, she heard his happy sigh when he finished. "This place kind of looks like it's got enough money to be all electronic, but we'll see if we can find any paper records anyway."

The interior doors were, thankfully, unlocked. Claire set her bag down and eyed Mr. Gary's cup of pens and pencils. She snagged two and tucked them into her bag, certain Justin would both approve and appreciate not having to buy her new ones.

CHAPTER 20

JUSTIN

Justin looked up from rifling through a filing cabinet. This trip had turned out to be more fun than he'd expected. Trashing a symbol of authority never failed to amuse him. His own high school years had been pretty good, of course, aside from the panic, desperation, therapy, and court battles. He'd met Marie in high school, at any rate.

Wanting to think about something else, he glanced at Claire and smirked. "I couldn't fit all of Missy's toys into your suitcase, backpack, and bag even if I wanted to. That's not counting her clothes and bedding."

"Yeah, well, a fire and a lack of spending money kind of has a minimizing effect on stuff."

He sighed at his own stupid insensitivity. Obviously, a system kid wouldn't have much. "Sorry." The files wouldn't sort themselves, so he returned to rifling through them.

"Yeah, me too." She hefted her pack onto her shoulders. "It's gonna be pretty cramped in your house, so it's probably for the best I don't have much stuff."

"We can build onto it."

"Don't you need permits for that?"

"Only if you care about it being legal."

She laughed. "Yeah, you're not exactly Mr. Rule Follower."

"I was." Leaning on the drawer, he gazed over at the blue blinds on the nearby window, seeing other times and places. Now he felt ready to share. "My mom killed herself when I was five, so it was just me and Dad. Without her there to teach him better, he did what his dad did. When I was seven, he hit me with a belt so hard I still have scars from it, because I stayed out after the streetlights came on and was covered in mud when I got back. He took me to the hospital. They asked me what happened. I told them. Dad said I made it up and had been out late doing who knows what. They believed him over me.

"At school, the teachers taught us that we could trust doctors, cops, and them, and to always tell them the truth, no matter what. If someone hurt us, we were supposed to tell one of those three kinds of people, and they'd do something about it." His attention slipped down to the files again. That incident at the hospital had only been the first of many and he had no desire to linger on the memories. "A boy's bound to develop a certain disrespect for rules and laws when things like that happen."

Claire said nothing for several minutes. "I'm sorry."

"No need to be. Marie's parents are really great people. When Marie got pregnant with Lisa, I freaked out a little bit and begged Jack to help me learn how to be a father. Last thing I wanted was to turn out like my old man." Or, for that matter, Father Bernard. Jack had saved him in a lot of ways. Then Kurt had come along and introduced him to a place where he fit in.

He finally found a folder with the right name on the tab and yanked it out to flip through it. "I still don't care much about the laws and rules and all that. Don't have a reason to." He lifted a large card and waved it in the air. "This has Brian Avery's address in it as part of his emergency contact information."

"Oh." Claire stepped to Justin's side, put her arms around him, and hugged him. "You seem like a really great dad to me."

"Thanks. I try. Not as hard as I used to have to, but it still takes effort." Surprised by the gesture, it took him a moment to return it. "Especially since I've got girls. Lisa completely stymied me for a good three years. Would it have killed the universe to give us a son first so I had time to adjust to the whole 'dad' thing? Or even the second time, to sort of soften the pink unicorn barf all over everything."

She choked out a laugh. "Sorry, can't help there."

"Maybe you can have boys in a few years and I can live vicariously through you. It better not be for at least five years, though." He gave her a stern glare. "It's nice in some ways to have a five-year-old kid at twenty-four, but I don't recommend it."

"Jeez. Yeah, Drew and I can wait, thanks."

He raised an eyebrow. "Drew? Who's Drew?"

"The guy who got you to the basement. He's the one that's always been there."

"Oh really." Pushing her far enough away to give her a stern glare, he grumbled in the back of his throat. "Redhead? Lots of freckles?"

"Yeah." She looked up at him, and her brow climbed. "Ease down, Dad. I don't need my virtue protected or whatever you're thinking there."

"I'm a Knight," he growled. "I protect my own. Drew had better watch himself or he'll end up with a fist in his face."

Claire chuckled. "Yeah, and that fist'll be *mine*."

Thinking back, he remembered her saying that she got suspended for beating some kid up. He laughed. "Fair enough." The principal had a notepad on his desk, so Justin copied the address down and put the file away. "We're going to need a map, because I don't know where this street is."

"Yeah, me neither. We can probably find one at a gas station or something. I'm sure no one will think taking a horse to one is weird or anything."

He sighed, recalling the last time he had to stop at one. "Great. Tariel's addicted to chocolate bars. She's going to pout if she doesn't get one."

CHAPTER 21

CLAIRE

"His wife has a nice house." Claire sat on the curb across the street, eating a slightly stale muffin whose origin she preferred not to know. The smell of chocolate wafted past her with every one of Tariel's breaths. From here, they could see the two-story, three-car-garage home with precise white trim and matching shutters. Two Hispanic men were trimming the shrubs and mowing the lawn.

Brian Avery probably grew up with a nanny, just like Claire had. She wondered if his ever made him feel a little weird. Stewy had occasionally given her the uncomfortable feeling he wanted to eat her, Hansel-and-Gretel style. The way Justin's face had tightened up when she'd told him about Drew reminded her of the way her dad had watched Stewy sometimes. Maybe her instincts had been warning her about the wrong thing.

Justin shrugged and tossed his apple core into a nearby juniper bush. "She's probably got a steady job, and I expect he pays her some child support too."

"Yeah, I guess. What are we going to do here when someone gets home?"

"Try to get Avery's address. See if there's any other information we can collect."

"Right. And what are the limitations of this? I mean, we're not going to kill anyone, right?"

Justin lifted an eyebrow at her. "Look, that cat was an ur-phasm in a cat shape and nothing more. Leaving it alive would have—" He sighed. "Probably not been so bad in light of what wound up happening, but I didn't expect that. I was concerned about it reporting back to a Phasm. They're kind of annoying too. Best to put them down when you see them."

"Oh." Surprised by his explanation, she blinked. "Okay. I wasn't referring to that, but okay. We're still not going to kill anyone, right?"

He held up a solemn hand. "I have no intention of killing any human beings at this, or any other, time. I'm also not fond of killing animals and only do it when I must. Tariel is less picky, but bends to my crazy notions of morality and such."

"Okay, cool. So what's the plan, then?"

"I think they call it 'shock and awe.' " He hopped to his feet as the garage door cranked upward and a car pulled into the driveway. "Go, Tariel."

The horse, who had been lurking behind them, shot away, headed for the house. Justin rushed after her. Claire rolled to her feet and also followed, amazed by Tariel's speed. Seeing it from the outside was different from riding on her back. She saw the horse flash a hoof in the way of the garage door, tripping the safety sensor and causing the door to stop and roll back up. Justin's cloak flapped in his wake until he reached the garage. He ran in, Tariel backed out, and the garage door trundled downwards. Claire arrived in time to see him yanking the car door open and probably scaring Mrs. Ex-Avery out of her wits, but not in time to interfere with the garage door shutting.

"Why didn't you stop it that time?" Claire grumbled. "Now he's in there all by himself, and it probably never occurred to either of you that Avery might have stuff protecting his house. He's a cop *and* a Knight, and this is where his kids live." She hustled to the front door and found it locked. "And there's probably neighbors watching who'll call the cops. Come on," she told the horse as she ran to the back gate.

It had no lock and she held it open for Tariel. Once the horse trotted through, she shut the gate behind them, in case no one actually had seen anything yet. As they hurried to the back door, branches of a thorny rosebush reached out and scraped Claire's leg and sock. She hissed from the unexpected pain and jumped away from it. Tariel kicked out with her front legs to stomp on the branches. Tiny red lines told Claire the mare wasn't invincible. Of course, she already knew that.

It would take more than a rosebush to stop Tariel. The horse stomped in the center of the shrub again with a whinny of defiance, then chomped at the air when the branches stopped shaking. She trumpeted her victory and Claire waved to hush her.

"Keep it down. Unless someone is coming. Then get really loud so we know." She tested the back door and found it unlocked. As she entered the house, she made an effort to be as silent as possible and shut the door behind her. The kitchen reminded her of her parents' house, with granite countertops and chrome appliances. Dad may have loved the outdoors, but he appreciated a nice kitchen too. The hardwood flooring didn't creak as she took tentative steps across it.

Brian Avery, sporting a fading black eye, dashed in from the garage. He skidded to a stop when he saw Claire. His mouth fell open and no sound came out.

"Uh." When Justin had brought her here, she never considered that she might come face to face with Brian. She also hadn't thought much about what she'd do here, or what she'd say the next time she saw him. As she stood in his mom's kitchen, her brain froze.

CHAPTER 22

JUSTIN

Things did not go according to Justin's sketchy plan. He hurried into the house behind the teenage boy who'd freaked out, ignoring the younger one still in the passenger seat of the car. He'd wanted Claire to stay outside, so of course she'd found a way in and now had the older boy distracted. Swooping into the kitchen while both teenagers stared at each other, he grabbed the boy from behind and pinned his arms.

"I just want to talk to you."

Snapping out of his confused stupor, the kid struggled and squirmed in his grip. "Get off me," he howled. Though this kid had some muscle on him, and knew how to fight, Justin outweighed him and had more experience.

Justin hauled the boy to the island in the center of the kitchen, then he shoved the kid's head down until his cheek smacked the countertop and held him there. One of these days, he needed to start carrying handcuffs. This kid would be much easier to handle with them. "Are you going to settle down, or do I need to get violent?"

"Stupid bitch, is this supposed to be revenge?"

Justin had no idea what that meant and looked to Claire for an answer. She snapped out of a stupor to glare at the boy. "Yeah," she said, seeming to warm to the idea. "Yeah! It totally is, you prick."

"That's not why—"

The boy growled. "*You're* the one who hit *me*."

"You're the one who decided the new girl needed to be bullied." Claire closed in on him, her face twisted into a snarl. "What's the matter, Brian? Hasn't any girl ever fought back before? Or do you usually just cover their mouth while they scream?"

"I'd never date a skank like you."

"I'd never—"

"That's enough!" Justin roared. "Claire, settle down and sit your butt in that chair." To his satisfaction, she did it, every step rigid and staccato. "I take it this is the boy you beat up?"

She glowered at Brian and gave a curt nod.

"Great." Of course the kid she'd beaten up was Avery's son. Nothing could ever be simple. "We're not here about that." Before Brian could say anything else, Justin pressed his face harder into the granite slab. "We're here because I need to know where your dad lives and which precinct he works out of. Somehow I doubt you're going to volunteer that information at this point. Which makes you kind of useless. Do you know what happens to useless people?"

Brian's eyes popped wide. "You're bluffing."

Claire's brow furrowed and her gaze fell to her shoes.

"Am I?" He picked Brian up again and threw him at the wall. For the sake of showmanship, he drew his sword. "You want to test me and see?"

"Don't. Please don't." Claire's voice came out smaller and more plaintive than he'd heard from her before. "His dad did that to me."

He turned to see her hugging herself. Brian took advantage of the moment to throw his shoulder into Justin's gut. Because he had no intention of stabbing the kid, Justin tossed his sword aside to avoid doing it by accident. He punched Brian in the face and wrestled with him until they wound up on the floor. Justin held him down with his knee on the kid's back. The string of obscenities spewing from Brian's mouth made Justin raise an eyebrow.

This had gotten completely out of hand. "Claire, go look for a filing cabinet and see if you can find divorce papers or something else that shows Avery's address. We'll figure out where he works on our own."

She fled the room. He turned his attention back to Brian, who'd stopped swearing. "So my dad used to beat me up. How about yours?"

The boy under his knee went still. "What?"

"Your dad beat the crap out of Claire, and from what she said, I gathered he was experienced at that. I'm wondering if he used you for practice. Or maybe your little brother? Your mom?"

Brian gulped. "Um."

"Ask your mom for help, Brian. Just tell her you need someone to talk to. Make it about the divorce. That's rough on kids. Nobody has to know."

"Justin?" Claire's voice echoed in the stairwell. "There's cops outside the house!"

"I guess your little brother has his own phone. Damn." Justin sighed and shouted to Claire, "Come here and let's go!"

Of the two of them, Claire needed to get away more. He'd survive if he got arrested, and Tariel would find a way to help him get free. Claire wouldn't. They'd try to take her locket away and either kill her when she freaked out, or sedate her to take it, which would then kill her.

Claire ran to him, clutching a piece of paper. "I found it."

"Good." He heard pounding on the door and knew they'd run out of time here.

"This is the police. Come out with your hands up!" a voice shouted through the door.

Claire had gone pale and he wanted to throw her out the door. "Run, Claire."

"What?"

He let go of Brian to reach Claire and shove her at the back door. "Get on Tariel's back and go!"

The front door crashed open and cops poured inside. "Freeze!" a uniformed officer shouted. "Put your hands up!"

Claire gulped and threw the door open. Justin raised his hands, standing where he blocked the cops from shooting her. Through the open door, he met Tariel's gaze and nodded to her. She'd get Claire to safety, whatever it took.

CHAPTER 23

CLAIRE

She thought the horse would wait for Justin, but as soon as Claire hopped onto her back and grabbed her mane, Tariel sprang away. Her last glimpse of Justin was of him getting down on his knees with his hands behind his head and watching her escape. Tariel jumped over the ten-foot-high fence, a feat she hadn't expected the horse to be capable of. They bolted up the street too fast for cops on foot to give chase and in the wrong direction for those still in their cars.

Holding on, her mind blanked by panic, Claire hunched down and shut her eyes against the wind. They moved so fast she thought a stray fly might kill her. When they turned onto a freeway onramp, her brain clicked into gear. "Wait," she screamed, trying to be heard over the roar of the wind. The horse slowed and hopped to a halt in the breakdown lane. "Justin didn't take me home for a reason. I need help, but not from Marie."

The horse snorted at her, and she got the impression Tariel had said "Then from who?" She rubbed her forehead, trying to think of an answer. Her social worker wouldn't be much help. Marie and the girls needed to be protected, not involved. None of her foster parents, former or current, could help. That left...Drew. She trusted him. He may not be useful, but he'd have her back, no matter what.

She took a deep breath and made the decision. "Take me to the group home."

Tariel turned her head to flash one skeptical eye at her.

Claire crossed her arms and narrowed her own eyes. "Hey, you never question any of Justin's plans, and he does stuff like slicing up doors in public buildings and rushing houses without expecting the cops to come. I'm at least getting the only backup available to me before storming a police station."

With a snort, Tariel pivoted and sped across the city. Claire jumped to the ground as soon as they reached the large house. "Back me up so I don't wind up in the basement again." That said, she walked up to the front door and threw it open. "Drew!"

Several heads popped out through doorways. Claire flashed them all a fake smile. Drew stuck his head out of his bedroom and her smile became real.

"What are you doing here?"

"Grabbing you. C'mon. Bring..." She shrugged. "We're gonna cause some trouble."

His red eyebrows lurched up. "I'm not sure that's a good idea."

The foster father thumped into the hallway, filling it with his girth. "I know that's not a good idea. You left. Fine." He crossed his arms. "You're not getting anyone else into—into whatever it is your costumed freak sugar daddy is into."

"Whatever. C'mon, Drew. I need your help."

"He's not going anywhere."

Tariel stepped up and stuck her head over Claire's shoulder. She bared her teeth and made a low, threatening noise in her throat.

Flinching away from Tariel, the foster father grabbed Drew by his shirt. "Get back, demon horse. You can't have this boy."

Drew gulped and stomped on his foot. As the foster father yelped and let go, Drew rushed out to wrap his arms around Claire. "This is the craziest thing I've ever done."

"Me too." Tariel sat her hindquarters down, and they scrambled onto her back. Claire grabbed two handfuls of mane and Drew held onto Claire. His hands groped more than she expected before they settled around her waist as Tariel broke into a gallop.

"Where are we going?"

"The downtown police station. We're going to rescue Justin."

CHAPTER 24

JUSTIN

The door opened and Avery walked in. He seemed cool and collected, and Justin nodded to him. "It's been a while."

"Yes, it has." Avery set a folder down on the table Justin had been handcuffed to. He crossed his arms and looked down his nose. "How's the wife? Last I saw you, there was a baby on the way?"

"Yeah, she's almost three now. The older one is five. Started kindergarten this year." Avery should already know these things, but Justin had let himself get wrapped up in his family. Everything with Mark's Phasm had happened because he'd chosen Marie and the girls over his job, when he needed to find a way to keep them closer to equal. The Knights needed him as much as his family did.

Avery's mouth twisted in annoyance. "I'm happy for you."

Looking around as if he'd never been inside an interrogation room before, Justin noted the faint smell of bleach. "I assume all the recording devices are conveniently broken?"

"Of course."

"What can I do for you, then?"

"Funny you should ask." Avery sat on the table with his body twisted so he could both see Justin and appear to ignore him. "Where's Claire?"

Justin shrugged. "Probably visiting the site of her family home. I imagine someone bulldozed the charred wreck and rebuilt there. It'll probably be upsetting, but she'll have to learn to live with it eventually. Did you ever find the guy who did it? I remember you saying you would."

Avery rubbed his side. Justin wondered if that spot had a scar, or if Claire had hit him there. "Yes."

"Good. Glad to hear it was taken care of."

"Got away." Avery bared his teeth in a snarl. "That bastard shot me and got away."

"Huh." Already lounging as casually as he could in the hard metal chair, Justin managed to get his hands to his face so he could stroke his chin in thought. "When was that? You know I would've helped if you asked."

"A few years ago." Avery waved dismissively. "It's not important. One Knight doesn't matter in the grand scheme of things."

Justin raised his brow and wondered if he should take that as a message about his own value. "Maybe, maybe not. His daughter kind of objected, though."

Avery rolled his eyes. "Always the bleeding heart."

"Last I heard, we take care of our own."

"Only when it's convenient."

"Only when we *know*."

Nostrils flared, Avery clenched his jaw. "Too late."

Justin doubted that a Knight who also happened to be a detective couldn't find someone if he tried. "We could hunt him down together. You and Mark were friends, weren't you? Don't you want to see his killer brought to justice?"

"The damage has been done, and there's nothing more to be gained by hunting it." Avery turned away from him, rubbing his eyes with a finger and thumb.

His use of "it" caught Justin off guard. From that one word, he guessed that some kind of Phasm entity had burned the house down and shot Avery. But that made no sense. Ur-phasms had to take animal bodies, which couldn't hold a gun and would have trouble setting a fire without alerting the family or Kupiri. Full Phasms couldn't affect the real world directly.

Without knowing why, it seemed important not to let on he'd noticed the slip. "But you know where he is."

Avery raised an eyebrow. "Why? Do you think *you* can handle it?"

Hope flared in Justin's chest. Avery may have been tainted, but he hadn't lost his mind. With luck, he could avoid having to break out of jail. "I'll never know until I try. Besides, is there a downside to letting me do your dirty work?"

"Yes." Avery stepped away from the table and went to the door. "But it might be taken care of later, so we'll see."

"Wait."

Avery's eyebrows quirked up, suspicion etched in every line of his face. "For what?"

Justin cast about for some way to get Avery to give him an opportunity to either do his job or free himself. He'd asked Avery to wait without knowing what to say or do next, and tried feigning weariness to cover his uncertainty. He needed to kill the corrupted Phasm, and to do that, he needed to get close to it.

This would be the first time he'd run across one, though he'd heard and read other Knights telling stories about their hunts. His biggest challenge would be figuring out how to get close to the Phasm without letting it seduce him. Avery could inadvertently help though, especially if he thought he could turn him.

"At least let me see Mark. He should know someone is looking out for his daughter."

Avery faced the door for several seconds, then said, "I'll think about it."

Icy dread settled in Justin's gut as he wondered what Avery would do in the meantime.

CHAPTER 25

CLAIRE

Tariel stopped a block away from the police station. Until this moment, Claire had been focused on getting here. Now, as she and Drew helped each other clamber down from the horse's broad back, her mouth went dry.

"Okay, we're here," Drew said. "How are we going to get Justin out of jail?"

Claire gulped. "I don't know. He'd know what to do. We need Justin to figure out how to break Justin out of jail."

"We don't have him, so we have to figure it out ourselves."

"Wait." Her gaze settled on the horse, who blinked one large blue eye at her. "Don't we?" Claire grabbed Drew's hand and plunged inside the station. She walked up to the desk and smiled at the woman in the blue uniform. "Excuse me, we're looking for my big brother. He was arrested earlier this afternoon, and we have his bail money."

The woman gave them a pitying smile. "What's his name?"

Claire blinked. He hadn't told her his last name, and she'd never asked. "I'm pretty sure it would be under Justin. Guy in chainmail with a cloak and sword?"

"Oh, that guy." She mostly stifled a roll of her eyes and a shake of her head. "He's down in Holding. First basement. Talk to the officer behind the desk down there."

"Thank you." Claire pulled Drew to the stairwell.

As they hurried down the stairs, he leaned close and asked, "We have bail money?"

"As if," she whispered. "C'mon. We're going to talk to him. Justin's going to come up with a plan to rescue himself." They breezed into the darker, dingier Holding desk area, with concrete flooring and no-longer-white walls. Drew put his arm around her shoulders while they waited in line, and she stared at the file cabinets, then the stacks of papers littering the desks. A long table against the wall held pamphlets for various types of counseling services, legal aid, citizenship, and the library. Above that, a bulletin board had notices in an array of colors about all kinds of community events and services.

The woman in front of them wanted to collect her husband's belongings. The officer denied her request on the grounds that everything would be held until his release. The exchange made Claire wonder how they'd retrieve Justin's armor and sword. Swearing up a storm at the officer, the woman left in a huff.

With a heavy sigh, the tall, black officer gave Claire and Drew half of his attention. The other half went to the black plastic binder in front of him. "What do you need today?" he said in a bored monotone.

"Hi." Claire gulped, suddenly nervous about lying to a cop. "Sorry to bother you. Um. My big brother was arrested earlier, and I was told he's down here in holding? The guy with the cloak and armor?"

The officer blinked at her and rolled his eyes. "Right. You're here for Sir Lancelot. Just visiting, or posting bail?"

"Visiting, please."

He opened the binder and pushed it forward, handing her a pen chained to it. "Print your name here and sign here. I'll need to see some ID."

"I have a school ID, is that good enough?"

"Yes."

She handed Drew her backpack, and he rooted through it for her ID while she wrote her name on the page. The officer looked it over and grunted. He pointed her through a door to a large room, told her the visit would be recorded and monitored, and called the next person forward.

Drew put his mouth next to her ear. "How are we going to get him to plan his escape if it's recorded and monitored?"

"I don't know." She forced herself to smile as she told the guard she'd come for Sir Lancelot. He directed them to one of the several metal picnic-style tables in the Holding area. Drew sat sideways and pulled her close. Her spirits sank further when she saw Justin—without his armor—led into the room with his hands cuffed and attached to a chain around his waist. His feet had been cuffed to that chain, also, and he looked cranky. Her smile faltered and failed.

"Get your hands off her," he growled at Drew. "You can keep them to yourself until we have a chat about appropriate behavior."

"Yessir." Drew lifted his arms in surrender.

With a smirk, a guard shoved Justin down onto the bench opposite them. "Fifteen minutes," he grunted, then left.

"Why are you here? Do you have a brilliant plan?"

Claire gulped. "We were hoping you'd have one."

"Mine went so perfectly, I can't see how another one could possibly fail." Justin rolled his eyes and sighed. "You shouldn't be here. It's not safe."

She stuck her chin out. "I can take care of myself."

"Avery's in the building."

"Oh." Sparks of fear flashed out to her fingers and toes. "I was worried about you. Tariel is too."

"I'll be fine."

He seemed so distant. Her shoulders slumped and she looked away. "I guess...I guess you kinda regret picking me up the other day."

"No." He sighed again. "Not even a little, and not for a second. Look, since you're here anyway, Avery—" He flicked his eyes past her shoulder, then he spat out the first swearword she'd ever heard him say. "Protect Claire and the locket," he hissed at Drew.

He lurched to his feet and charged despite his chains. Claire turned to watch in stunned horror as he plowed into Avery and he two men tumbled away from the door together. She grabbed Drew's hand and yanked it, pulling him to the exit. They raced out together, hit the door for the stairwell, and ran up.

"Where're we going?"

"I'm not sure!" Claire burst through the door to the ground floor and snapped her head back and forth in a panicked rush to see everything at once. Cops turned to stare at their unexpected entrance. She blushed and shuffled to the front door again. The thought crossed her mind that Avery might have files on Justin at his desk that she could destroy. He'd be busy downstairs for a while, and she might not get another chance to do it. Besides, Justin had been about to suggest something. Based on what she knew of him, it had to have been an idea like hers.

She whirled and marched to the front desk again. "Excuse me. Um, where can I find Detective John Avery's office?"

The woman raised an eyebrow at her. "Third floor."

"Thanks." She walked to the stairs again, trying to project calm purpose and not alarm anyone. When she reached them, she ran up with Drew on her heels. On the third floor, she recognized the hallway to the side. It had the closet they'd used to see her dad. Drew pointed her to a secretary beyond it, who directed them to Avery's office and said they could wait there for him.

The room had a metal desk surrounded by filing cabinets, plus files stacked on the desk. It had no personal items, not even a single picture. Nothing but files, files, and more files. Claire shut the door behind them and frowned. "Jeez. How do we even start looking?" She noticed Justin's sword in its sheath behind the door and picked it up. He'd need that.

"He's probably got a system." Drew went to the desk and picked up the top file of a stack. "Hey, this one is for that weird theft at the Historical Society museum. It has a picture of Justin."

"Yeah." Claire scanned the room. Seeing no labels, she picked a drawer at random and slid it open.

"What are we looking for?"

"Anything else with Justin in it." She ran her fingers across the files, finding each had been labeled a single word and a date. These dates were all from ten to fifteen years ago. Dismissing that drawer, she moved to another one and flipped a finger across the dates. Nothing of interest.

On her sixth drawer, she stopped at a folder marked "Terdan" with the date her family's house had burned down. Finding it here surprised and stunned her. Her first social worker had told her the insurance company classified the fire as an accident and set up a trust for the payout that she'd get access to when she turned eighteen. Why would a cop have a file for an accidental fire? She pulled it out, opened it up, and laid it on the desk. Drew, with two files in hand now, peered over her shoulder as she flipped through the pages.

This file painted a different picture than the one she'd been told. It had a report from an arson investigator and another from a crime scene investigator. Concerned that Avery might return at any moment, Claire skimmed the notes and documentation until she found summaries of their findings. Both declared the fire "most likely" to be arson. She brushed her finger across the signatures, feeling the indentations from a ballpoint pen that meant these must be originals.

Underneath those, she found photocopies of reports from the same two names, both also signed. These two reports had completely different data and notes, and the summaries indicated the fire had been an accident. More pages below it turned out to be handwritten notes. Her eyes picked out the word "Knight" several times, then she noticed the word "Phasm."

Drew touched her shoulder. "Why would he have the reports faked?"

The more she read, the more she furrowed her brow. Justin hadn't explained enough about Knights and Phasms yet for any of this information to make sense. "I don't know. I think so he didn't have to suppress how the fire really started. I could be wrong, because his handwriting is a kinda crappy, but I think he thought a Phasm killed my dad."

"A what?"

"I'll explain later."

"Okay." He put an arm around her to show her the file he'd found. "It looks like he's been building a file against Justin for a while. There's notes from stuff in Salem, Olympia, Seattle, Eugene, and another thing in Portland. Dates on his notes show he's been putting it together for about two and a half years. He doesn't have a last name or any idea where to find him, so he hasn't picked him up yet. Not sure why he didn't just enter Justin's picture in the system and let the other cops find him."

She flipped through the file, which had few official papers of any kind and only two pictures of Justin. "Not enough evidence, probably. Besides, he wanted me to do something specific, and I bet he wanted Justin to do it first. So he builds up a case, then arrests Justin and says he'll make that all go away if Justin just does what he wants. I wonder if he's trying the same thing right now, or if he's got all his hopes pinned on me already."

"What a whackjob."

"Yeah. I guess maybe he wasn't always one, since he had a wife and all. Justin called him 'tainted.' I wonder if someone can be *un*-tainted." She wondered more if a Phasm could be un-corrupted.

"We should probably get out of here." Drew snatched both folders away and tucked them under his shirt.

"Yeah."

Chapter 26

Justin

By the time other cops waded in to stop the fight, Claire had disappeared. Justin kept as much of a hold on Avery as he could for as long as he could, to keep him busy. Hands pried them apart, and he felt a line of hot blood dribbling out of his nose. To his satisfaction, Avery doubled over, clutching his gut and panting.

So much for trying to convince Avery to return to the Knights. It had been worth it, though, to give Claire a chance to get free. Later, he'd tell her how proud he was of her for thinking of him, even if her plan had been stupid, incomplete, and fraught with far too much danger for her own good. He spat in the vicinity of Avery's shoe, missing by an inch or two.

"Get them both to the infirmary," someone barked.

In the infirmary, he stood a chance of getting himself free in a much simpler way than the one he'd have to use in a jail cell. Justin went limp and considered the best place to fake an injury that would get his hands loose. He groaned and curled around his wrist.

"I'm fine," Avery growled. "Watch him."

"Just let them check you over, Detective," someone said. "You're bleeding."

Two large men picked Justin up and shoved him around until they reached a first aid suite. It had everything necessary to deal with minor injuries, including a woman in a lab coat. One cop thumped him in the chest to make him sit on the gurney.

"I think my wrist is broken," he whimpered.

Avery glared at him. "He's lying." Another cop had helped him shamble down the hall and set him in a chair. "Faking it."

"We'll see." The woman in the lab coat waved at the handcuffs, and one cop unlocked them.

With his hand now free, Justin surged to his feet and slapped the doctor so hard her whole body twisted. He dropped a shoulder and shoved it into the cop's belly, managing to catch his solar plexus with the blow. The cop dropped to the floor, wheezing, and Justin grabbed his keys.

"See? Faking." Avery leaned forward, a palm pressed to his head.

Keys in hand, Justin punched another cop in the face while the third pulled his gun. He ducked behind the woman and wrapped an arm around her neck.

She slammed a syringe into his thigh. "You guys are all the same," she said with a disgusted sigh. Her thumb jammed the plunger down, filling his leg with numb heat.

As much as he hated to do it in front of normal people, Justin took a deep breath and called on the bond he shared with Tariel. The woman crossed her arms and waited for the drug to take effect. Disappointing her would make his day, but seeing Avery doing the same thing with his sprite ruined the feeling. Regardless, Tariel's peculiar brand of power washed over him, burning away the drug and all his pain. He tightened his grip and circled to put the woman between him and both the gun and Avery.

"You're not going to get away," Avery growled.

"I'm willing to risk it." Justin dragged the doctor out of the triage clinic with the cop and Avery echoing his every step down the hallway. His sword would help a lot right now. So would his horse. He backed through a fire door, kicked it shut, and shoved the woman against it. With only one hand free, he had to use his body to hold her there as he unlocked his other hand and the chain around his waist. Thumping on the door told him he needed to hurry.

The woman watched him over her shoulder, eyes wide with frightened wonder. "How did you shrug that shot off?"

"Magic. I swear this is nothing personal, and I sincerely hope you'll be fine." He punched her in the back of the head, hard enough that she clonked into the door, then passed out. Hopefully, she'd wake up in a few minutes.

The pounding on the door stopped, and he suspected they knew a way to circle around behind him. He unlocked the chains on his feet and shucked them. Shoving the woman out of the way, he opened the door again and ran to a stairwell he'd seen on the way here. He hurtled up it, knocking someone aside, then burst out on the ground floor, where he saw Tariel taking up half the lobby with no Claire or Drew in sight.

Claire had had the option to walk out the front door and didn't take it. She had to be wandering around inside the police station someplace, which meant Avery would find her. He scowled, turned on his heel, and marched back into the bowels of the building. He headed for Avery's office, a place he hadn't visited in years.

He tossed the stairwell door open on the third floor and stepped out as Avery walked out of the elevator. They each changed direction to intercept the other. Justin threw a punch; Avery ducked and threw his own. Justin caught him with a foot to the knee; Avery slammed him into a wall hard enough to dent it. While Justin recovered, Avery threw a fist into his gut. Justin stumbled back.

This fight, he reflected, would be much easier with his armor. Avery had too much more skill and experience, and the cop would win if he couldn't find some advantage. Justin blocked a kick with his forearm, then he charged Avery, jamming his shoulder into the other man's chest and sending him tumbling over a desk.

"Justin!"

He snapped his head to the side and saw Claire standing in the doorway to Avery's office, holding his sword. She tossed it. The sword was made from his own will and powered by his connection to the Palace. Though he couldn't make it appear in his hand from anywhere, he could catch it by the hilt without looking. Swinging the silvery blade around, he took a defensive stance and watched Avery clamber back to his feet. Avery's eyes darted to Claire, and Justin sidestepped to put himself between them.

"Claire, could you lock yourself in his office for a minute, please?"

"Uh, sure."

Avery scowled and raised a baseball bat. "It's time to settle this."

"We could sit down and sing Kumbaya instead. Roast some

marshmallows together."

"Or I could beat you to death."

"That doesn't sound like fun to me. How about rock-paper-scissors?"

Avery answered by rushing him. The bat worked well enough, though Justin recalled Avery being most comfortable with a gun. It hadn't been on his hip in the interrogation room, or later in the visitor's area of the holding cell level. He'd probably left it in his office. Now Justin had him blocked off from that. Thank goodness, because a bullet would kill him without his armor.

The sword hit the bat with a thunk, hacking a small chunk of wood off. Justin gave a foot then took a foot, then pressed forward and was driven back, all the while chipping pieces off the bat with every strike. They ranged in an arc around the office door and Justin worried he'd be worn down before Avery lost the fire in his belly that goaded him to continue.

He'd have to take a chance and hope for the best. With his left hand, he threw a punch at Avery's head and took a thump to the side from the bat. It hurt, but compared to the crap his father used to do, it was nothing. Emboldened by that thought, he ducked to the side of Avery's swing, let him smash the bat into his thigh, and punched Avery's face with the hilt of his sword.

Avery stumbled back, grabbing his nose, and Justin ignored the burning pain in his leg to stick with him, clocking Avery in the neck. The detective crumpled to the floor, and Justin hit him again for good measure.

"Claire!" The space, while clear now, would probably fill up with people soon enough. The office door opened and Claire popped her head out. Grabbing Avery by the hair, he asked her, "Which closet was it?"

Chapter 27

Claire

"Uh." If she chose to be honest with herself, Claire had to admit she'd expected Justin to lose that fight. The sight of him triumphantly dragging Avery by his hair confused her enough that she stopped and stared.

Drew nudged her. "Are you okay?"

"Oh. Yeah, I, um, it's that one over there." She pointed and took two steps toward the closet door before turning around and kissing Drew. He hadn't yet figured out what to do with his hands when she let go and looked into his eyes. "You did great, but you need to get someplace safe."

"Huh?" He shook himself. "What about you?"

She wanted to explain that her father waited for her in that closet, but nothing came to mind for how to accomplish that both in few words and without sounding insane. "I have to go in. Get out of here, at least, before someone comes to arrest you." Hearing the closet door open, she ran for it to make sure Justin didn't leave her behind. Her shoe stopped him from shutting the door on her, and she darted inside and pulled it closed.

"Claire, this is too dangerous." He dropped Avery on the floor and rubbed his side.

"There is no way I'm letting you go kill my dad by yourself."

"He's not your dad."

"I know." She hoped she could still believe that when she looked into his brown eyes. "I need to go. Please let me go."

Justin sighed and rubbed his face. "This goes against my better judgment."

She raised an eyebrow. "What do you think your judgment is better than? A tomato, maybe?" When he glared at her, she held up her hands in surrender. "Sorry, sorry. Look, I get that you're kind of a double whammy of mentor and adoptive dad, and that probably makes you the most protective Knight ever. But I *have* to do this. I *have* to face him. It's important to me. Please?"

He stood, raising to his full six feet and change, and seemed suddenly much more impressive in jeans, work boots, and a T-shirt than he had with the cloak, armor, and horse. The sword in his hand helped. "Keep your head down and eyes open. You matter to me."

Her belly flushed with warmth and belonging, and she hoped she would never let him down. Words would sully the sentiment, so she nodded and squared her shoulders.

Echoing her nod, he waved her off and gripped the door handle. Later, she'd ask him to explain what he did while he had his back to her.

When he opened the door, the darkness rushed them again, and she saw him move his head in quick, sharp jerks to take it all in.

"What's this? A gift?" Her father's voice resonated in her chest. It called to her, pulling her to the source.

Justin put out a hand and stopped her. "Gift?"

This place felt warm and safe and more like home than any other she'd ever known. She wanted to curl up and forget everything and everyone else. "I know you need help, Daddy." She ducked under the obstacle in her way and scurried deeper into the darkness until she found him.

Her father gathered her into his arms and held her. "Welcome to my demesne, Knight."

"Let her go."

Claire turned to see that Justin had followed her. "It's okay." The words felt right and wrong at the same time. She frowned and pulled away enough to look from one man to the other. Both would protect her. They ought to agree about what to do.

"Claire, remember what I told you."

She tried to remember where she'd been a minute ago and couldn't. Her father's arm held her close and she inhaled, hoping to be soothed by his scent. Instead of the smell she remembered, of cedar, musk, and damp earth, she got nothing.

"There's no need for a sword here, Knight." With her ear pressed to her father's chest, she heard his every word as a rumble in her bones. It made her want to cling and ignore anything that might contradict him.

"I think that's probably not true. I mean, Avery tried to kill me, and he's your tainted Knight. As it turns out, I'm not ready to be best pals with anyone whose pet swings a baseball bat at my head."

"He's often overzealous in his efforts."

"Yeah." Claire's voice felt distant and breathy, as if her mouth opened and someone else spoke for her. "He can be forgiven."

"It comes from all his years as a cop, I'm sure," Justin said. He sounded so sour and hostile.

Behind him, Claire heard Avery groan. He'd be fine soon, then Justin would leave, one way or another. Once he left, Daddy would take care of her. Wait, she didn't want to be taken care of. Not like *that*, anyway. She wanted to have a home, a place full of love, laughter, and light, not a sanitized prison. She wanted to see Drew, and to finish high school. Words could hardly express how much she wanted to have her room in the Palace to retreat to if she needed time to herself.

It hurt to think. She pushed away from her father but his grip tightened. "Daddy, I want to sit."

"Not now, Pumpkin. Remember that time we went to the park and you wanted to sit in the mud? I stopped you so you wouldn't get your pretty pink dress dirty."

"If you remember that, you must remember your house burning down?"

Justin's even, reasonable voice cut through Claire's confusion. Her house had burned, and so had her parents. This version of her father held nothing but memories. He had no future, no dreams, no hopes.

"Of course. There was a..." She looked up at her father and saw him frown. His eyes slid down, and he let her go enough to touch the locket under her shirt. "I gave you this." Tugging at the chain, he lifted it out and let it dangle in the air. The moment he saw the pendant, he let go of Claire and seemed to forget about her.

"An ur-phasm came for me, sent by a corrupted Phasm to taunt me. It took so much from you..." He rubbed his thumb over the filigree and furrowed his brow. "I couldn't kill it, only drive it away. I don't remember why. We were at the park? You were so small. I took you to the hospital, and they said you were dying."

"So you made the locket to save her. It replaced her lost essence with power from the Palace." Justin spoke softly, his voice gentle and soothing.

"It became a ne-phasm. Kurt and I killed the Phasm, but the ne-phasm got away."

"And then it came back," Justin said, "years later, stronger than before, and set your house on fire, hoping to get revenge and the locket in one fell swoop. Kurt had retreated to the Palace by then, so it had only you to focus on. It tried to kill Avery when he figured it out, but instead, you arrived in the middle and sheltered him in return for his fealty."

Claire stared as Justin laid it all out. At the same time, panic roiled in her gut. He had her locket, and she feared he'd take it from her. Her hands shot up to grab the chain. Why did she wear it on something so thin and flimsy? It should have an unbreakable wire to keep it safe. "Daddy, you have to let me go."

His hand curled around the locket in a fist. "Yes, you can go. But not this." He yanked the chain hard enough to make her squeal, and the clasp broke.

She stumbled back as Justin surged forward. Unable to find her footing, she fell. Avery raised himself up on his hands and knees, glaring at Justin and swiping his hand through the air for a weapon. Darkness closed around her, and she wondered if she'd ever hit the ground.

CHAPTER 28

JUSTIN

His heart stopped. Justin had only known Claire for a few days, but in that time, he'd already warmed to the idea of adding her to his family. Her own father's corrupted Phasm had killed her, in front of him, and he'd never wanted anything more than he wanted that thing to die. Charging it sword-first, he focused on taking it down. Everything he felt would only get in the way right now.

The Phasm raised a sword of his own and metal clanged on metal as it sidestepped his rush. The Phasm's blade had a fancy golden basket hilt, making it a copy—no, a *mockery*—of Mark's real sword. This thing had just murdered the daughter of its own body, and now it dared to invoke Mark's noble past.

In the name of justice, he could set aside grief for a brave, spunky girl he barely knew whose life deserved to be much, much longer. The

Knights, on the other hand, had been a part of his life for years. He'd met dozens of honorable men who carried the banner, and strove to emulate them. He'd gotten help and advice when he needed it most, and hadn't had enough time to repay Kurt for everything.

With a roar of rage, he flashed his blade through the air. Steel flashed and clanged as the Phasm met every blow. He drove it back, though, and kept it on the defensive. His anger fueled him past the point when he should have tired, keeping his arms quick and legs strong. He knew he had no hope of outlasting a being made of what could be called magic. As with Avery, he needed to let his opponent hit him. Tariel would call it a dumb idea, and she'd be right.

He gritted his teeth and lowered his guard. The Phasm stabbed him and, as Justin had hoped it would, left itself open to a counterattack. Before he could seize the opportunity, something slammed into Justin's knee from behind and drove him to the ground. He glanced over his shoulder, and saw Avery, his face already healing over. The Phasm tossed Avery a sword, one different from Mark's or Justin's.

In a moment, carelessness had cost Justin this fight. He never should have assumed Avery would stay unconscious, and definitely should have tied his hands to something. If he somehow managed to survive, he'd never make that mistake again.

"I remember meeting you a few times, Justin." The Phasm flicked its sword away and turned its attention to the locket dangling from its fingers. "You were brash and young. And stupid. It's nice to see you haven't changed."

Avery held his sword against Justin's neck. "Hand it over." He pointed to the blade still in Justin's grasp.

"What if I don't?"

"Then your wife gets to become a widow."

Justin gulped, thinking about the wringer that would put Marie through. The girls were so young that they'd manage. Marie, though, would be devastated. "And what if I do? I just want to have a clear picture of my options here. It's always best to know the fine print before signing a contract."

Avery snorted. "Oh, please. Do you expect me to believe you'd give up being a Knight? You're practically their poster child for how everything can go right."

The Phasm held up a hand. "Now, John, let's not be hasty. There's no reason to discount him. He could be a valuable ally. He's certainly strong and capable, and he's so young. You're not going to live forever."

Rolling his eyes, Avery pressed the blade tighter to Justin's throat. "You can pledge your fealty to Mark."

He'd hoped there would be an option other than death or outright betrayal. "How will you destroy the Palace if I pledge my fealty now?"

Mark laughed, and the stars overhead flared in time with it. "We have the locket. Avery can get into the Palace anytime he wants." He tossed the necklace to Avery.

Avery's sword went slack as he turned his attention to catching it. Grabbing a piece of the Palace out of the air should be easy, except for someone who'd repudiated it and bared his soul to a corrupted Phasm. Sparks of adrenaline shot through Justin's body as he realized this would be his one and only chance. He put every ounce of effort he had into throwing his sword at Mark.

Surging to his feet, he forced Avery to choose between catching the locket and defending himself. The moment of hesitation and confusion allowed Justin to slam his fist into Avery's jaw from below, knocking Avery unconscious again. Justin whirled and caught the locket without looking, in time to see Mark staring, dumbstruck, at the sword through his chest.

The Phasm might be able to recover. Justin leaped to his side, grabbed the sword, and slammed it in deeper. As he shifted his grip to rip it to the side, Claire whimpered. Both Knight and Phasm turned at the sound.

"You bound her?"

Mark blinked rapidly, fondness overcoming his features. "She's my daughter. I couldn't just kill her."

"I'll take care of her. I promise." Justin tossed the locket, and it landed on Claire's chest. She sucked in a deep breath.

"I know you will."

Maybe a corrupted Phasm could atone or be cleansed, or whatever the right word should be. They'd never know, because Justin wouldn't take the chance. He ripped the sword out and carved up Mark's Phasm with a blade designed for the task. "Rest well, Mark."

CHAPTER 29

CLAIRE

Claire's eyes opened in time to see Justin slice up the Phasm that had once been her father. It had no blood or guts. The body dissolved, and so did the night sky. She wrapped a hand around her locket as Justin scooped her up into his arms.

"This might hurt a little," he said.

They fell. He landed on his feet in the closet and stumbled on office supplies, then crashed through the door. Through it all, he held her and kept her safe. He landed on his back in the hallway and groaned. She wound up still clutched in his arms and draped over his chest. His sword clattered to the floor, sliding a few feet away. Cops and clerks, startled by their sudden appearance, rushed toward them.

Avery groaned and flailed in a pathetic attempt to get to his feet.

"It's Sir Lancelot."

"He escaped earlier!"

"He's got a weapon."

"Hands where we can see them!"

All the voices scared Claire enough that she slid off Justin and hid behind him as he sat up.

Justin raised his hands in surrender. "This has all been a grand misunderstanding." He turned to check on Avery, and so did Claire. She had no idea why Justin thought Avery would help them now, but if he did, then so did she. The guy had been knocked for a loop, though, probably by Justin's fist, and wouldn't be offering them any excuses anytime soon.

For the second time, she heard Justin mutter a swearword. He turned and whispered to her, "Claire, you should go. Tariel ought to still be here. I'll...catch up."

"Are you crazy?"

"Probably. Just fake a good cry and run for the stairs."

She hadn't faked a cry in a very long time and didn't need to now. Being still for five seconds gave her enough time to think about everything that had happened with her father's Phasm and how much she wished he could have been something special after death, instead of something awful. She did, however, have to fake noisy sobs as she scuttled away with tears in her eyes and ran for the door.

In the stairwell, she kept running, afraid someone would chase her down and demand explanations. Bursting out on the ground floor, she fled straight to Tariel who still stood in the lobby despite several people trying to tempt her out with apples and other foods. The horse's tail twitched and she shoved someone aside with her nose while stealing an apple.

Relief flooded her. Claire dodged between the people and threw herself at the horse as impatient and incredulous voices bombarded her with too many questions and demands. Somehow, between the horse rolling her shoulders and pushing with her head, Claire wound up on Tariel's back and held on to her mane while the mare darted out of the police station.

Outside the glass doors, Tariel reared up and flashed her front hooves out, discouraging anyone from following her. She landed with a jarring thud on the sidewalk, then shot up the street.

"Justin's coming!" At least, she hoped he was.

CHAPTER 30

JUSTIN

Three cops hurried after Claire as she fled the closet. With all the people in the room, Justin knew the cops wouldn't shoot unless they had a clear shot. However, they could probably catch Claire. He hopped to his feet and tripped one, then threw his body at another. The two of them slammed into the third. "I wish I could let you interfere, but I can't." He glanced back and saw Avery hadn't recovered yet. With Mark's influence gone, the detective would need to spend some time putting his head on straight. Pushing him now would only make Avery's next few weeks harder.

Several voices wanted him to stop, shut up, and get down on his knees with his hands behind his head. He sighed and wished things could be simpler. Later, Avery could straighten all of this out. Or the guy might have lost his marbles, leading him to blow his brains out. Justin preferred the former, but it wouldn't happen until Avery had a chance to collect his scattered wits.

A few years ago, it had taken Justin two weeks to learn to step on his sword, flip it into the air, and catch it. Every second he'd "wasted" on that ridiculous skill paid off now, when he stomped down and wound up with the hilt of the blade in his hand. The cops, even those with their guns out, stared, and he liked to think it had to do with how impressive his display had been. In reality, he suspected they wanted to avoid hitting their fellow officers who currently littered the floor around him in various stages of standing up.

He hopped to the side, slammed the blade into the wall and slashed down to make a quick hole. He cut another wall and rushed through it, then another, until he found the outer wall of the building. Gunshots followed him as he ran at the window and thrust his sword into the only thing left standing between himself and escape. Without slowing, he threw his body forward and shattered the glass.

Three floors from the ground, he had time to reflect on how much hitting the road would hurt as he sailed through the air surrounded by chunks of safety glass. He landed feet-first on a police car with a grunt, denting it and rolling off the side to hit the ground less gracefully. More gunshots made people on the streets scream and scatter, and he scrambled to his feet with a groan.

Pain shot up his right leg. "Any time, Tariel," he muttered. "I could really use an exit right about now."

"Drop the weapon and put your hands up!"

Glancing behind him, Justin saw an arm with a gun poking out of the window of the car he'd landed on. "Really? Now? And here I thought everything would be easier with Mark out of the picture. But no, it's just getting worse. Thank you, Portland. You're now officially my least favorite place ever." He glared at the arm. "Pull that back in or I'll chop it off before you can fire. I just cut a hole in a window with this sword. A couple of bones aren't going to be a problem. I'm just trying to get home to my family, for heaven's sake."

The cop in the car gulped and his arm wavered. "Uh, no, you need to drop the sword."

Knowing he'd regret it, he smacked the gun with his elbow and knocked it aside. It fired and he felt a sharp impact in his side that he'd have to heal whenever he could scrape a minute together to relax. For now, this fresh pain drowned out all the tiny cuts and less tiny bruises to sing a harmony of agony with his leg. The gun clattered to the street, and he spared a moment to kick it under the car. No random idiot on the street should be able to pick it up from there.

To his immense relief, Tariel rounded the nearest corner and pounded up the street to him with Claire on her back. He slashed his sword through the car's front tire and hopped around to face her. When she reached him, he gritted his teeth and grabbed her mane. Her power swirled around him, guiding his foot to the stirrup and lifting him off the ground. He focused on not stabbing either her or Claire.

Landing on her saddle jarred every bone in his body, and he cried out from the pain. Claire reached back and groped a hand over him until she found a belt loop, then held on. Her well-intentioned effort jerked his body, grinding the bullet in his side against his ribs.

Before Tariel could reach full speed again, a crow dove at them from above and managed to scrape Claire's scalp. She shrieked. Justin clenched his jaws together and curled around her. When it dove again, he used his head by smashing the side of his skull against the bird to stun it. The crow fell before he could catch it, and Tariel's hooves trampled it.

"Get us out of here," he growled.

The horse sped up, carrying them away from sirens, shouting, and screaming. Running like this took too much of Tariel's power for him to heal before they stopped. At least she knew he needed it. Stupid cops had to take away his stupid armor. If he'd had it, that gunshot would've only grazed him and left a bruise. Instead, he now had to worry about bleeding to death.

As far as he knew, he hadn't done anything bad enough to justify the cops requesting help from Vancouver's finest. That meant he only needed to keep a firm grip on consciousness until they crossed the state line. Every hoof hitting the street jarred him enough that he worried he might not last that long.

CHAPTER 31

CLAIRE

Confused and terrified, Claire glanced back repeatedly to make sure Justin was still breathing. When they found him, he had a bloodstain spreading on his shirt and a wretched grimace on his face. Even with that, he still leaned over to protect her when that demented crow tried to rip her head off. One hand holding her head, the other firmly lodged in Justin's belt loop, she tried to shoulder some of his weight.

To her horror, the hand wrapped in Tariel's mane went slack and he bounced, then the two of them slid off Tariel's back and hit the ground at high speed. She tumbled and rolled, scraping her hands, elbows, and knees on the asphalt. Winding up flat on her back, she stared at the puffy clouds skimming past. Darker ones loomed to the west, promising rain soon.

Screeching snapped her to the present and she groaned. Several feet away, Justin lay in the road, not moving. The noise had come from cars, braking hard to avoid hitting him. Thank goodness they'd seen him. Claire rolled to her hands and knees, which hurt, and forced herself to crawl to his side.

"No, you can't die." She curled both hands in his blood-soaked shirt and shook him feebly, willing him to wake up. Too many things had forced her to shed too many tears, and she refused to let this be yet another. "It's not allowed. You're going to be my dad, you said so. I'm going to have little sisters and a place to stay forever. Wake up, you big dope!"

Voices around her asked stupid questions. Someone put a hand on her shoulder. Someone else tried to nudge her away from Justin. She clung to him and couldn't tell if he breathed or not. A shrill whinny rang out, and everyone scattered. Tariel's head reached over Claire's shoulder with a squirrel wriggling in the horse's teeth and chittering up a storm.

Justin groaned and his eyes fluttered. Through clenched jaws, he said, "Did anyone get the number of that horse?"

More relieved than she'd ever been about anything, Claire threw herself across his chest.

He grunted. "Ease up, Claire. It takes time to heal. And shut that stupid ur up, it's going to drive me nuts."

Sitting up, Claire wanted to scowl at him but couldn't stop a smile from leaking through. "You big dork. I thought your stupid butt died from falling off your horse."

"If I died, rest assured it would have been from getting shot." Wincing, he eased himself up to sit with a hand on Claire's shoulder. "Are you alright?"

She wiped her nose. "More or less. We're in the middle of the street."

"I just need another half a minute here." He leaned on his elbows, making tiny noises of pain. "And I need that—" He grunted something unintelligible. Claire thought it might have been him biting back a curse word. "—ur to shut up." Tariel brought the squirrel closer to him, and he grabbed it out of her mouth. "Give me one good reason why I shouldn't lop off your head right now."

Claire looked around and saw people watching them. Some had their cellphones out, taking pictures or video. "I can think of a reason." She gulped. "It might be on the Internet in thirty seconds if you do."

CHAPTER 32

JUSTIN

"Crap." The pain faded away as Tariel healed him. He spotted his sword lying in the gutter. Aware of how awful he must look, he hopped to his feet and gave Claire a hand up. Because he had an audience, he paced to the side of the road, stomped on the sword's hilt, and caught it. Several onlookers obliged him by gasping at the feat.

"What're you gonna do to that squirrel?" A spindly young man with dreadlocks and patched jeans crossed his arms and gave Justin a suspicious glare.

He looked down at the ur-phasm, grateful it had finally shut up. It looked up at him and gulped. "You could just let me go," it said.

None of these people would believe that the thing in his hand had tried to kill Claire and devour her essence. "I think my horse hurt it. I'll take it to a vet and let them check it over." His stupid sheath had been left behind at the police station with his stupid armor, which meant he now had to keep a hold on the sword.

Both hands full, he vaulted himself into the saddle with two fingers. Claire had to climb up on her own, and he watched her wince from what must be dozens of tiny scratches and fresh bruises. He fervently hoped she'd get to the Palace soon so she could attract her own sprite and let it heal her.

As soon as they both settled, Tariel launched into a gallop up the street. "Now," Justin said to the squirrel, "let's have a chat. I'm sure nothing bad will happen to you if I let go while we're moving this fast."

"C'mon, I'm not hurting anyone."

"Only because I stopped you."

"I can't help it if she's tasty!"

Justin rolled his eyes. "Who do you work for?"

"Nobody! Just a free—*glrk!*"

He wanted to squeeze until its eyes popped out, but restrained himself to get information. "Try again."

It gasped and wheezed as he eased the pressure off. "Terlizzi. Its name is Terlizzi."

Justin flushed, remembering when that cat-shaped ur-phasm an eon ago had let "ter" slip. At the time, he'd assumed it meant "Terdan," as in Mark, Claire's father. It had never occurred to him there might be another corrupted spirit to deal with. If he'd known then, he would have gotten backup.

"Where can I find Terlizzi?"

"I don't know." When Justin squeezed again, it flailed. "I swear! It's not tied to a demesne. It roams, like a person."

He'd never heard of a ne-phasm that could roam wherever it wanted. Of course, he'd never asked about details like that. Maybe all the other Knights knew. "What does it look like?"

"Skinny. Short. Compact."

As Tariel pounded over the I-205 bridge, he provided as much shelter for Claire as he could without his cloak and tried to think of anything else that might help locate the ne-phasm. Nothing came to mind, as it sounded like the thing had no preferred hunting or lurking area more specific than "Portland." Rather than give this ur a warning or let it scream, he used a quick, sharp jerk to cut the thing's head off and flung the body at the water.

"Take us home, Tariel." Though Claire still represented a risk to his family, they couldn't avoid the house forever. At least she could grab a decent meal while he left her behind to visit the Palace. Spending the night in Avery's care probably hadn't included much in the way of food.

He noticed Tariel turn her head enough to give him a long, slow blink. She *should* feel guilty for letting him fall off her back. Her power *should* have been strong enough to hold him in place, even when he passed out. At the worst, she should have stopped and come back before Claire had a chance to freak out. The kid had been through more than enough already over these past few days. He pulled her closer and rested his chin on her head. With luck, she'd be able to spend some time relaxing and coming to terms with her new life.

CHAPTER 33

CLAIRE

The ride ended too soon. Claire wanted to stay wrapped in strong, warm arms forever, with no disasters or pity intruding. Justin already meant so much to her, which bothered her a tiny bit. Getting close to Drew had taken months, but only a few days ago, Justin had swept into her life and made her want to be a part of his family so much it ached. Then again, if Marie hadn't turned out to be the sweetest person ever, she might not have latched onto him so fast and hard.

Tariel stopped in front of the farmhouse. This place would be her home now. They'd find space under their roof for her and share their joy with her. She hoped they'd let her crash in Lisa's bed tonight instead of on the couch, because spending last night in a cold, empty cell left her craving companionship. Drew would suit her better, just to hold and be held by someone who wanted her, but the little girl would be her sister. That fact warmed a whole different part of her heart.

"I'm going to stop in and let Marie know I'm here, and then I need to go to the Palace," Justin said as he helped her down. "Whenever you get there, by the way, my room is 557, on the fifth floor. Go there as soon as you can, because I won't know your room number until you tell me. I'll show you around and help you figure things out." He pulled her suitcase and bag off Tariel's saddle, where both had somehow managed to remain lashed down all this time.

"Okay." She nodded and wiped her face. It felt dirty and gritty, and so did the rest of her. The last time she'd taken a shower seemed like *ages* ago. A hot bath might be even better. She hoped she wouldn't screw up their routines too much. "Five-five-seven. I'll remember."

He smiled then sighed and herded her up the path to the cottage. "I just realized there'll be four women in this house now. I think we need another bathroom."

She grinned, not quite ready to laugh yet. "If Drew stays with us too, then..."

His brow quirked up. "He can—" Peering at the cottage, he frowned and cut himself off. Dropping Claire's suitcase, he stuck his arm out to stop her. "Something's not right. Stay close."

Taking her own look at the small house, Claire saw nothing amiss. The garden still looked bare, the path still had mud, the wood-chopping clearing still had an axe and wood. She trusted Justin and his judgment, though. He'd more than earned it. Staying quiet as she strained to see whatever he'd noticed, she followed him to and through the front door.

When he wiped his feet on the mat, she did the same. He tossed the inner door open and filled the space with his body. His back and legs tensed, and she watched his knuckles turn white as he tightened his grip on his sword.

"Welcome home, Knight." The cold voice froze her heart.

CHAPTER 34

JUSTIN

What Justin saw made him want to dive in and kill things. Marie and Drew both sat at his dinner table, tied to the chairs and gagged with duct tape. At least it hadn't gone to the farmhouse and taken the girls from Jack and Tammy. Marie had been crying long enough to make her eyes red and her cheeks blotchy. That she wore her best red nightie sent guilt coursing through him.

He'd intended to come home and properly express his affection and appreciation for her. Instead, he'd ridden off to return the hat, then rescued Claire. That could have waited a couple of hours. This might not have happened if he'd come here first.

Drew had been roughed up. He had a black eye now and a spritz of blood on his shirt. His glasses lay on the table, one lens cracked and the frame bent out of shape.

"As you can see, we waited for you ever so patiently." The short, spindly, man-shaped ne-phasm wore a hood, putting his face into shadow. It stood far too close to Marie for comfort.

"What do you want, Terlizzi?"

Its face lifted enough for him to see the sneer on its thin mouth. "So you know my name." He caught a flash of steel as it whipped its hand around to settle a knife under Marie's chin. "Goody for you. That won't save your precious, delicious wife." It ran its fingertips up her arm.

If not for the knife, Justin would have tossed the table aside to rip its arms off. "Take your hands off her or I'll do it for you."

"You'd like to, I'm sure." It pushed the knife against her neck without breaking the skin. "Humans are so disappointingly fragile. I'd almost like a fight to take your essence."

"I'd be happy to give you a fight. Put down the knife, and let's take this outside." He tried to signal with a hand behind his back for Claire to leave before it noticed her. She'd have a better chance against this thing if she could surprise it.

It chuckled. Then it sniffed the air. "Wait. What's that behind you? It smells...familiar."

Justin swore.

CHAPTER 35

CLAIRE

That name, Terlizzi, reminded her of someone. Claire racked her brain, trying to think of how she knew it. His voice tugged at her memory too. She wanted to see his face. Uncertain what Justin's hand gesture meant, she moved closer, hoping to glimpse the person threatening Marie. Pressing her face to the door jamb, she managed to find a sliver of space to peer through with one eye.

Seeing Drew crushed her. If not for her, he wouldn't be in this situation. She hated what she saw of Marie too. With difficulty, she forced herself to look away from their horror to see their captor. Though she could only see his chin because of his hood, she recognized him without being able to place him. Where had she seen and heard him before? When he tilted his head to get a better look at her, she saw his beaky nose and a brown eye.

She furrowed her brow in confused recognition, wondering why he, of all people, would do this. "Stewy?"

Justin shifted so she could see better while still standing in front of her. "You know him?"

"Stew*art*." He scraped the hood away, revealing his full face. Claire remembered him as a clean-cut young man, perhaps twenty years old. This version of him had creases in his face and white patches in his scraggly beard and hair. He'd aged forty years in the span of only six.

Letting her mouth fall open, she stared in disbelief. "What *happened* to you?"

Stewart scowled and loosened the knife at Marie's throat. "Your stupid essence, Claire, that's what. Your essence gave me everything. Suddenly, I could leave my master Phasm's embrace. I roamed for a while. Found a nascent Knight and devoured him. Ate a few other people. But I needed something they couldn't give me. Your dad stopped me before I could get all of your essence." He spat on the floor.

"Without that last piece of you, I couldn't grow. I found this idiot and took his shell. It was easy by then. I got your mother to hire me as your nanny. But then! Augh, your dad did something and your essence was locked away. So I stayed and I watched and I tried to puzzle it out. In the end, I tried to kill you, but that didn't work either. Because you escaped somehow."

As he spoke, his face twitched, and his eyes narrowed more and more until she wondered how he could see her. "And you disappeared. Vanished. Gone. That cop Knight found me and thought he knew something. He didn't. I shot him, and then I watched him. He fell so hard. I kept tabs on him, and he tried to figure out more about Justin.

"Then, just a few days ago, some of my urs found a strange, tasty morsel when she stepped off safe property for more than five minutes. I've been looking for you since then, Claire. Thanks to Drew here, who burst out of the police station and ran up the street while I was nearby, I figured out what Avery couldn't—where Justin lives. So. Here we all are. Isn't this nice?"

Claire noticed his knife hanging limp in his hand and figured Justin would see it too. If they could get Stewart away from Marie, Justin could leap in and skewer him. She pushed on Justin's side, and he let her through with a frown. No matter how he felt about her plan, though, she knew he'd protect her.

"Here I am," she said. Clearing the doorway, she held her hands out for Stewart and tried to keep them from shaking. "You want it, come and take it."

Stewart's mouth and nose twitched in a pout. "I already know I can't. I just told you. There's something in the way."

Her mouth dry, she pulled the locket off her neck. She had to clench her teeth together and focus with all of her will to let it dangle from her fingers. "How about now?"

His eyes widened, and his gray tongue slid out between his lips. "The last piece," he breathed.

Claire hoped she survived this dumb idea.

CHAPTER 36

JUSTIN

The moment he figured out Claire's plan, Justin went still. His job for the next several seconds involved being forgotten by this thing that called itself Stewart. Someplace, maybe under the couch cushions, he could probably find a quarter. With it, he would be willing to bet that Kurt had slain a corrupted Phasm named Stewart shortly before Justin had found his way to the Palace.

He watched Stewart's face betray its naked lust for Claire's essence. It stepped away from Marie. Justin tensed, waiting for the perfect moment when it got far enough away not to threaten his wife anymore, but before it got close enough to Claire to attack her. Time slowed down for him. Each footfall took forever. He heard the faucet dripping. Marie sagged against the duct tape binding her hands. The locket swung back and forth through the air.

Justin charged, sword-first. It had worked on a window, so it could work on a ne-phasm that had somehow managed to get itself into a human form. It batted his blade aside with more strength than he expected, and Justin crashed into Stewart without stabbing him. They tumbled to the floor together, Justin's hand smacking painfully into the couch's wooden frame on the way. His sword bounced and slid across the floor. Stewart surged with a grunt to pin Justin on his back. Justin grabbed Stewart's wrist to keep the ne-phasm from plunging its knife into his chest.

"Claire, run!" He heaved to the side, forcing Stewart to stab the floor. The knife dug an inch into the cheap linoleum and the plywood underneath. Using the momentum of the roll, he threw a punch at Stewart's face. To his great surprise, the ne-phasm cackled and sent them spinning until they hit the wall.

Somehow, Stewart kept a grip on his knife. The ne-phasm slammed it down again, this time arcing its arm around to plunge the short blade into Justin's side. It pulled the knife out and rocked to clamber off his body. Justin ground his teeth together against the pain and lurched off the floor, catching Stewart's ankle before it could scamper away.

Claire stepped into the fray, her face painted with rage. Amazed and awed by her courage, Justin watched her swing a chair at Stewart's head. It clipped the ne-phasm in the shoulder, stunning it. Justin heaved himself onto the ne-phasm's legs and held it in place while Claire slammed the chair down on its head.

"This is for my father," she growled. Stomping a foot on its chest, she said, "This is for my mother." She dropped to the floor in a pro-wrestling-style move to drive her elbow into its chest. "And this is for my brother!"

Stewart squealed and grunted. With a swell of pride, Justin judged Claire to have the ne-phasm under control for the moment. He dove for his sword and curled his fingers around the hilt. In the time it took him to do that and spring back, Stewart managed to recover enough to grab Claire and roll her into the couch, pinning her there.

With a flash of bright white light, Claire disappeared. Stewart's arms held empty space. It scrabbled to its hands and knees. "No!" Patting the couch as if it'd find a secret door or compartment, Stewart made panicked, wailing noises.

Justin let out a sigh of relief. "She's out of your reach now." Her door would be a couch, the lucky little snot. She'd be able to find one in any house, furniture store, or breakroom, and even restaurants and bars. Rising to one knee, he shoved his sword through Stewart's back. The ne-phasm never saw it coming and stared down at the blade sticking out of its chest, arms falling limp at its sides.

"No," it whimpered. "This isn't how it's supposed to be."

"Don't care." Justin dragged the blade to the side and hacked at it again. This thing would never harm Claire—or anyone else—ever again. It painted his home with blood, but they'd survive, and the girls could stay at Jack and Tammy's until he and Marie cleaned it up. Sagging under the weight of exhaustion caused by a very long day, he sagged to the floor and took a deep breath.

"I'm sorry," he said to Marie as he pulled on Tariel's power to heal yet another injury. Energy surged from his sprite to him, making it possible for him to stand. He grabbed a steak knife and cut the duct tape holding Marie's hands together. She threw her arms around his neck. He held her while she shuddered with tears that he thought came more from relief than anything else. "I'm going to let you get the tape off your own mouth so you can keep it from hurting too much. I have to cut Drew free."

As soon as Justin loosed him, Drew ran to the couch, sucking in panicked gasps. He ripped the tape off his mouth with a high-pitched shriek, then groped the couch frantically. "What happened? I don't understand any of this."

"It's okay. She's fine." Justin stepped to his side and squeezed his shoulder. "We'll find a way to explain later. Right now, I have to go get her."

Marie had ripped her own tape off with a whimper and now rubbed an ice cube over her mouth. "Come home tonight, no matter what."

"I promise. Drew, go wash up in the bathroom and don't come out until my wife is dressed." He kissed Marie's cheek. "I'm sorry this happened, and I'm sorry I didn't come back right away. Kurt died. It seems like it happened weeks ago, but it was today. Now Claire is a Knight, and I have to keep anyone from gutting her for it."

Marie nodded and hugged him. "Get something to eat there. I'm going to clean up and go to bed. Wake me when you crawl into bed tonight."

"I will. I love you."

"I love you too. Get going." She slapped him on the butt.

He snorted. "Put on a robe or something, woman. That's a teenage boy in the bathroom." He picked up the hacked corpse by the hair and found it unexpectedly light. Using a towel as a sling, he collected all its parts in one load and took them out into the woods. He preferred dealing with Phasms and ur-phasms—they dissolved when they died. This thing got blood and gore everywhere, and he'd have to bury it properly later.

For now, he dumped all the disgusting pieces in a pile as he hurried to his sycamore, hoping Claire hadn't riled up the whole Palace already.

CHAPTER 37

CLAIRE

Claire hit hard stone and tumbled into a wall. The bare, empty square confused her. Justin had said it would be a bedroom, a place where she could rest and be safe. A bedroom should, she thought, have a bed. It could also have a dresser, some shelves, maybe a lamp. The room did at least have enough light to see by, though she saw no obvious source.

Staring up at the ceiling, she noticed all the aches and scrapes and pains from falling off Tariel and stomping on Stewart. Justin...had to take care of that. If he didn't, then she'd never find anyone to adopt her. After the past few days, she couldn't go back into the foster care system. She'd stay here. But first, she needed to know if Justin was okay.

With a groan, she used the wall to help herself stand. The room had its own private bath and toilet. It needed towels and toilet paper. She pulled the front door open and stared at it. From the inside, it appeared to be a regular wood door. The outside confused her until she touched it. Couch cushions exactly like the ones at Justin's house made up her door, with the number 462 emblazoned in green at her eye level. She touched the numbers and discovered they had been made from tiny bits of crushed stone.

Scratching her head over such strangeness, she stepped into the long, stone hallway and had no idea which way to go. Picking left for no reason other than a desire to find Justin's room, she walked down the corridor. The other doors she passed each had a different design, for both the doors themselves and the numbers on them. She passed several kinds of stone, wood, metal, and even a blue plastic patio table. The creepiest door by far reminded her of an ornate headstone.

At the end of the hall, she found a stairwell and climbed up one floor. Three men, all big and beefy like Justin, stood on the landing of the fifth floor, blocking the entrance. They turned to acknowledge her, then stared and blinked and stared some more.

She gave them a weak smile. "Hi, um, can I go through that door, please?"

"What are you doing here?" The dark-skinned man had a thick accent.

"I'm a Knight?"

"That's ridiculous." The second man had an Australian accent. "How did you get here?"

She bit her lip and wished Justin would hurry up and get here to fix this. "I, um, don't know?"

The door opened behind them, and they moved for another man to walk through. She took the opportunity and slipped past them. The doors started at 501 here. Behind her, the men—now four of them—gave chase. She fled from them, checking numbers until she found the wood door inlaid with two silver fives and a seven. Rattling the knob, she discovered it was locked. The four men caught up to her as she pounded on the wood and tackled her to the floor.

"Let go! I'm a Knight, you have to let go." One of them grabbed her foot and she kicked out with it, hitting him in the face. They all paused for a heartbeat, maybe surprised by her well-executed kick. Then someone sat on her legs, and someone else clocked her across the jaw.

CHAPTER 38

JUSTIN

Opening his door, Justin found four Knights clustered in the hallway. Three of them he only knew in passing. The fourth, Djembe, tossed Claire over his shoulder. When she offered no resistance, he realized she must be unconscious. He frowned and reached for Djembe to stop him.

"What's going on?"

"This girl somehow got in here."

"She's a Knight."

The four other Knights gave him similar expressions of disbelief and alarm. Justin wanted to laugh at how comical it seemed. Seeing they were quite serious, he stifled it.

"Girls can't be Knights." Djembe stalked away.

Justin followed him, and the other three trailed along behind them.

"How else could she possibly have gotten here?"

"I don't know, and I don't care. I'll take care of it." His ground-eating stride brought them to the stairs.

Justin hurried to catch up and grabbed his arm. "Whoa! Djembe, wait. You can't just kill her." He thought he knew how things worked here. Apparently not. There had to be a way to protect Claire, and he racked his brain to figure it out. Kurt would know, but the bastard had to go and die this morning. "At least convene a convocation about it. Have elder Knights weigh in. Let me stand on her behalf."

Djembe raised an eyebrow at him. "You know this girl." When Justin nodded, Djembe's lip curled. "Fine. Let's go. But girls don't belong here, brother. You're on the wrong side of this."

Pressing his mouth shut, Justin followed him. He needed the time to tamp down his outrage and figure out how to explain the situation. Besides, an argument in the stairwell would be overheard. Opinions would be formed. Claire would die.

They reached the bottom of the stairs and strode out into the Great Hall. The magnificent chamber boasted pure white marble, crystal-and-diamond chandeliers, and frescoes from every time period since the inception of the Knights, all preserved in their original bright colors and precise designs. Djembe strode to the far end, where a large metal disc hung from the wall.

Djembe tossed Claire without regard for how she'd land. Justin caught her and checked her pulse as he eased her to the floor. Her heartbeat felt strong, at least. What his fellow Knights had done to her sickened him. Worse, if he'd delayed another few minutes, they would've already killed Claire. After the last few days, she deserved so much more than that.

When Djembe thumped a fist into the center of the gong, Justin heard a quiet metallic thunk. Along with every other Knight in the Palace, he felt the sound reverberate inside his chest. Claire shifted and groaned, and he brushed her cheek.

"Aren't you married?" Djembe towered over him, scowling with his thick arms crossed over his chest.

"Yes."

"Where I come from, we honor our women, not betray them."

"Don't," Justin growled.

Djembe snorted and curled his lip again.

The room, large enough to hold all seven hundred Knights at once, filled with men from all corners of the world. Several arrived with food in hand, others dripping wet and wearing only towels or robes. Nearly a hundred men formed a crowd around Justin, Claire, and Djembe.

"Brothers," Djembe's deep voice boomed, "a witch has infiltrated our beloved Palace. We must expel her before she teaches her dark sorcery to others."

Dark rumblings ran through the crowd.

"She's not a witch!" Justin rose to his feet, glaring at Djembe. "This girl is Mark Terdan's daughter. He was a Knight. One of us. It may be strange and unprecedented to have a female Knight, but that doesn't mean it can't happen." Judging the audience to be listening, he launched into the story he'd pieced together from both the ne-phasm and Mark's Phasm.

"Several years ago, a Phasm left behind by a Knight named Stewart became corrupted. It sent an ur after Mark, and the thing managed to get at Claire, who was then just a small child. It took most of her essence before Mark interrupted it and failed to kill it. He found a way to replace her lost essence with power from the Palace and forged it into a locket for her.

"Mark and Kurt hunted the Phasm down but never found the thing that nearly killed Claire. It became something strange, different from a usual ne-phasm. Left unchecked, it grew powerful enough to possess a human body while also becoming obsessed with what remained of Claire's essence. It convinced Mark's wife to hire it as their nanny.

"Whatever Mark did to create the locket and bind it to Claire prevented the thing from devouring the rest of her as long as she wore it. When Mark got suspicious about its behavior, it killed him and his family by burning his house down. By a quirk of luck, Claire happened not to be there and it lost track of her.

"John Avery investigated the arson and found the ne-phasm. When he confronted it, the ne shot and nearly killed him. That shooting took place near enough to attract Mark's Phasm, which caused its corruption and Avery's tainting. Both the ne-phasm and Mark's Phasm have been dealt with. Claire was instrumental in that effort and showed at least as much courage and resolve as any other Knight."

Given how much blood and pain the whole incident had caused, it took less time to relate the story than he thought it should. "She's here because of Mark's actions. Our brother couldn't stand the thought of losing his daughter, and we owe it to him to at least let her try to shoulder the mantle."

Djembe, still scowling, stepped past him and held his arms out to speak to the crowd. "Mark did something wrong. He should never have saved her in the first place. Even if he had, he should have killed the ne-phasm before it grew strong enough to kill him and the rest of his family. I say we take the locket from her and return the power where it belongs, in the Palace."

"Because you want to watch her die? She's just a kid, like you were, like we all were when we started here."

"She's a girl, and this was done without permission or consideration for the consequences. It was a great mistake."

On the floor, Claire stirred and her eyes fluttered open. Justin crouched beside her and helped her sit up. "Look at her, all of you. What he's talking about is killing her, finishing the work of a ne-phasm instead of giving her a chance to prove herself. There's no law that says a girl can't be a Knight. What's more, no one noticed the power Mark siphoned off. We still wouldn't know he'd done it if she happened to be his son instead of his daughter."

Djembe crossed his arms again and turned his back on the crowd, still scowling. "This is madness," he snapped.

"I agree." Until now, Justin had considered Djembe a friend. He curled his hand into a fist and readied himself to throw it if he needed to defend Claire physically. Around them, angry voices simmered. Justin couldn't tell if anyone stood with him or not.

Rondy slammed his sword into the floor. The clang echoed in the hall and everyone quieted. "Boys, we can resolve this without fighting." He turned a kind smile on Claire. "Young lady, do you want to be a Knight?"

Rubbing her jaw, Claire took Justin's help to wobble to her feet. "I didn't get the feeling this job was voluntary. Either you do it or you get killed."

Pride swelling in his chest, Justin beamed and refused to try to hide it. "She knows more than I did when I got here, but not by much. We've been busy."

"The biggest problem I can see," the elder Knight said as he paced forward, "is that the locket can be taken away. May I see it?"

Claire gulped. Justin put his hands on her shoulders and squeezed. She pulled the locket out of her shirt and held it up.

Rondy brushed a finger across it. "Unless the more heartless of you youngsters want to overwhelm Justin and myself, there will be no murdering of this girl for the crime of having the 'wrong' genitals."

Justin let out a sigh of relief, and the tension ran out of Claire's shoulders.

Someone called out, "Does that mean I can finish my shower?"

"Yes, go ahead. All of you who aren't interested in meeting our newest Knight right now can go." Rondy stroked one of his gray dreadlocks.

The room emptied again. Justin watched Djembe and a few other Knights fix him and Claire with glares offering promises of trouble in the future. He sighed and put it out of his mind as something he couldn't fix right now.

Looking to Rondy, he asked, "Is there some way we can, I don't know, transfer the power from the locket to her person? Having it in a separate object nearly killed her once already. If we can prevent that for the future, I think we should."

Rondy nodded. "I think so, yes. I have no idea how Mark created this in the first place, but that was the hard part. Between the three of us, we'll be able to manage the transfer."

With the last hurdle overcome, Justin hugged Claire. "That's great."

Claire returned it. "For a minute there, I thought I'd have to punch someone in the face."

Justin chuckled, glad she could crack a joke. "Thanks, Rondy. I should have come to you sooner. Everything just happened so fast."

"What's done is done." Rondy smiled down at Claire. "I think you're going to shake things up around here. I think maybe that's a good thing. If you ever need anything and he's not around, you can come to me."

"Thanks." Claire hugged Rondy.

Justin watched her connect with another Knight and found it satisfying. She'd find her way, and she'd be fine, though she had her work cut out for her in proving her competence to Knights like Djembe. He and Rondy would watch over her until then.

CHAPTER 39

CLAIRE

"This is the official paperwork." Justin set the manila folder in front of Claire and sat down at the table with her. "Avery seems to have smoothed everything over, so I had no trouble getting them to accept me. I'm a happily married, upstanding citizen of Washington State, have a place of residence, and passed their minimally useful psych test. Since you're over age fourteen, for this to be final, you have to sign it."

Marie stood at the sink, washing dishes, and Lisa and Missy played with toys on the floor. Drew also sat at the table. Claire opened the folder and scanned the pages. She'd never seen official adoption papers before and wanted to savor the moment. Justin and Marie had already signed them. As expected, his signature was a messy scrawl and hers was perfectly legible with classy loops and swirls.

He set a ballpoint pen on the paper and clasped his hands, watching her. "Before you sign that, I think we should discuss some rules."

She gulped. "I thought you didn't like authority figures."

"I don't like them exercising authority over me." He smirked. "I'm fine with being one."

"Oh, I see how it is." She already had a room of her own here, which somehow had come together over the course of two days. They'd found a spare bed for her, and Justin had thrown some shelves together. With his help, she'd build the rest of her own furniture. She hadn't had her own room for six long years. "What kind of rules?"

"Thing is, it wasn't so long ago that Marie and I were teenagers. We did some extremely stupid things."

Marie grinned over her shoulder. "He means that he did some extremely stupid things. I only did a few mildly dumb things."

"Thank you, dear."

Claire giggled. "Um, okay. So what're you looking to prevent?"

He shrugged. "Pregnancy, drug use, prostitution, death, the usual. Since we don't have a phone here, it'll be hard for you to call when you want to do things, and I'm not saying you can't go out and do things. We just want you to be as safe as being a Knight allows. And no getting naked with Drew until you're confident about being ready and all that."

Drew blushed crimson. "I, um, I don't think—"

"I've been a seventeen-year-old boy, Drew, and it wasn't that long ago. Don't even try."

With a gulp, Drew nodded and looked down at the table. "Jack already said I'm to sleep in my own bed every night. By myself. Until we're both eighteen."

Justin smirked. "Then Jack and I agree."

Claire bit her lip and wished she could frame this. Being accepted and even welcomed into this family meant a lot. This moment in particular showed her so much that she really fit in here. Justin would be firm but not strict, and Marie would temper him with humor. If she got into trouble, of any kind at all, she could come to them and talk about it. He'd never lock her in a basement or take away anything she held dear.

"Aside from the sleeping arrangements, are any of these *actual* rules?"

"Do they need to be? I can say 'be home by dark' if you want. I'd rather trust you to use your best judgment and try to let us know when you won't be around for dinner."

She broke into a grin. "That works for me." Picking up the pen, she sighed with pure happiness. She signed her first legal document with no reservations.

Justin pushed the folder aside. "Girls, Claire is officially your big sister now."

Missy squealed with delight and both girls jumped up and ran to attack her with pink and purple and unicorns and hugs.

"To celebrate," Marie said, "Grandma and Grandpa have cake. We can go over there whenever we're ready."

"It's okay, Drew. You can kiss her. Just keep your hands to yourself." Justin's last few words came out with a bit of a growl to them.

Claire laughed and let her new family embrace her. Whatever else might come, she knew she had a place to call "home." Finally.

Other Books by Lee French

Maze Beset trilogy

Superheroes in denim

Dragons In Pieces

Dragons In Chains

Dragons In Flight

Fantasy in the Ilauris setting

Damsel In Distress

Shadow & Spice (short story)

Al-Kabar (coming Fall 2015)

Spirit Knights

Young adult urban paranormal adventures

in the Pacific Northwest

Girls Can't Be Knights

Backyard Dragons (coming in 2016)

The Greatest Sin

Epic fantasy series co-authored with Erik Kort

The Fallen

Harbinger

Moon Shades

www.authorleefrench.com   www.myrddinpublishing.com

About the Author

Lee French lives in Olympia, WA with two kids, two bicycles, and too much stuff. She is an avid gamer and member of the Myth-Weavers online RPG community, where she is known for her fondness for Angry Ninja Squirrels of Doom. In addition to spending much time there, she also trains year-round for the one-week of glorious madness that is RAGBRAI, has a nice flower garden with one dragon and absolutely no lawn gnomes, and tries in vain every year to grow vegetables that don't get devoured by neighborhood wildlife.

She is an active member of the Northwest Independent Writers Association, the Pacific Northwest Writers Association, and the Olympia Area Writers Coop, as well as being one of two Municipal Liaisons for the NaNoWriMo Olympia region.

www.authorleefrench.com   www.myrddinpublishing.com

Myrddin Publishing

unique electronic & print books

Young Adult Fantasy and Science Fiction from Myrddin Publishing

Alison DeLuca

"Alison DeLuca is a master storyteller who deserves much more recognition than she gets. This is Steampunk adventure at its best!"

The Crown Phoenix

Steampunk adventure series

Nightwatchman Express

The Devil's Kitchen

Lamplighter's Special

The South Sea Bubble

Gypsy Madden

"This has all the elements of Buffy, Charmed and a host of other excellent magical series. Ms Madden's characters are well developed and she writes the sort of lean, muscular prose I love to read!"

Paranormal thriller

Hired By a Demon

www.authorleefrench.com   www.myrddinpublishing.com

Gary Hoover

"Gary Hoover does a great job describing this world, creating a vivid picture in the reader's mind."

Land of Nod

Dimensional travel science fiction series

The Artifact

The Prophet

Ross M. Kitson

"Talk about a creative mind! Ross Kitson has written a non-stop, action filled adventure that defies a genre label!"

Steampunk adventure

The Infinity Bridge

unique electronic & print books

www.authorleefrench.com   www.myrddinpublishing.com